ANGRY MOVIE GUY

★★★

IZZY CHURCH

SQUARE MONKEY PUBLISHING
New York

Angry Movie Guy
www.angrymovieguy.com

Copyright © 2015 Square Monkey Publishing
Library of Congress Cataloging-in-Publication Data
All rights reserved.
No part of this book may be reproduced or transmitted in any form or by any means without written permission from Square Monkey Publishing.
For information address
Square Monkey Publishing Rights Department
info@squaremonkeypublishing.com

For information about special discounts for bulk purchases please contact

Square Monkey Publishing Special Sales at 1.347.781.5539

For more information about how you can bring a Square Monkey author to your event visit our website at www.squaremonkeypublishing.com or call 1.347.781.5539

Cover Designed by Third Culture Creative
www.3rdculturecreative.com
Cover Photograph by Rachel Esterday
Printed in USA
First Edition: February 2016

ISBN (978-0-9964995-0-7) (pb)

Brazoria County Library System
401 E. Cedar Street
Angleton, Texas 77515

Dedication

For My Parents

Table of Contents

Acknowledgements	vii
Preface	ix
Introduction	1
Chapter 1	6
Chapter 2	15
Chapter 3	36
Chapter 4	52
Chapter 5	77
Chapter 6	104
Chapter 7	115
Chapter 8	135
Chapter 9	144
Chapter 10	158
Chapter 11	175
Chapter 12	192
Chapter 13	232

Acknowledgements

I want to offer my deepest gratitude to a long list of friends, associates, and contributing artists who without their advice, reassurance, and guidance there would be no book. Thank you to all who participated in the *Angry Movie Guy* stage reading: Director, Daniel Ademinokan, Actors, Brian Pracht, Seamus Dooley, Sarah Shaefer, Ian Kerch, Kevin Janaway, Dy Almeda, Ken Caphrey, Mellissa Rhyane, Jean Noel, Kitty Henderson, Amir Levy, Linda Hendrick, John Mourice, Traci Redmond and Ana Lucia.

Thanks to James Taylor for making sense out of nonsense. John Rogers and Max Waldbaum for their guidance. I would also like to offer my warm regards to my copy editor and line editor Otis Forbes and Jason Arnold for bringing their wit and insight to the book. Thanks to Marten Kayle and Caitlin McCormick for proofreading and editing. Their insight and keen eye for detail was an essential part of completing this book. I would also like to acknowledge *Third Culture Creative* for conceptualizing the cover design, as well as photographer Rachel Esterday and graphic designers: Albert Btesh, Rocky Baltazar and Israel Caraballo III for working on several cover designs. Additionally, I would like to acknowledge Maya and Cora for their contribution on the cover design. Thanks to George Campbell for being my model and allowing me to tie him up for the cover art. You're a trooper George!

Lastly, I would like to offer a special thanks to my Mother for proofreading and to my parents for their support and encouragement.

PREFACE

I came up with the concept for *Angry Movie Guy* while I was studying at Marymount Manhattan College. My major was communication arts and my academic specialization was writing for film and television. *Angry Movie Guy* was not an overnight success, but rather an arduous practice of learning that writing is re-writing.

I will confess the practice often had me going stark raving mad. More often than not, I was left begging for mercy whilst banging my head up against a wall. In hindsight, this was a childish and pointless endeavor since it became increasingly clear that I was pleading for sympathy from a God that was either deaf or at best hard of hearing.

Nevertheless, as arduous as the journey was to complete my first novel, it was indeed a literary voyage worth taking. If I were asked to do it all over again I would most certainly rise to the occasion. By sticking with the act of writing, I refined and honed my craft. Furthermore, I gained the confidence I needed to write my second romantic comedy titled: *Letters to Ganesh*.

In addition, I had the luxury of receiving counsel from a very long list of friends and associates who without their support and guidance I would have certainly given myself a lobotomy with a grapefruit spoon before ever completing this book. Thankfully… I live to tell the tale of a man named Charlie Zimmerman who only wants one thing: to be a well-regarded movie critic. Charlie relentlessly pursues his wide-eyed dream of becoming a movie critic, unwilling to budge, even when every door is being slammed in his face. Desperate to prove himself worthy Charlie transforms into the *Angry Movie Guy* in hopes of escaping the hypocrisy that has become his life.

I hope you enjoy reading *Angry Movie Guy*; it is a quirky and romantic love story, which I encourage you to share with all your loved ones, especially those lonely souls who are having trouble meeting that special someone.

Introduction

A beautiful slender redhead walks into a theatre accompanied by a dashing and admiring middle age man. They smile and greet the groups who have gathered for the screening. They quickly take their seats as the lights go down and the introductory score fades into the opening scene and eventually into the mellow dismal voice of the narrator who begins… only on two occasions in my entire life can I recall being astounded and resultantly speechless. The first time was as a result of my mother's unexpected death. She was struck with a debilitating disease that took her life in less than a week leaving me dumbstruck and distraught.

My mother was a famous actress, her death was highly publicized and her funeral was a mob scene. It was overcrowded with weeping fans and the news crew who wanted to capture the sense of loss we all felt. At the time of her death, she was in the midst of filming what might have been her greatest role ever. She was playing the pregnant wife of a German Jew. In the film, she and her husband are sent to separate Nazi concentration camps, however both of them survived the ordeal unbeknown to the other. Twenty years later, after both she and her husband had gone through hell and back, their son, who had relentlessly researched and tracked his father's footsteps against all odds, miraculously reunites them. The film was titled, *Till the End*, sadly, it was never released out of respect to my father and because he paid the studio half of our family's fortune not to release it.

My father was devastated when my mother died. She was his first love; he planned to grow old with her. My mother's sister, Hilda, thought what was best for my father was to give him some space to recover. Consequently, I was carted off to my rich and eccentric aunt Hilda's house in the countryside.

At the time, I was a chubby and insecure ten-year old boy who seldom spoke. I was left standing in my Aunt Hilda's driveway wondering if my father would ever return. My Aunt and I prayed daily for my father's speedy recovery and ten years later our prayers were answered. My father reverted to his normal self; it was not without the help of an attractive younger woman whose name escapes me, as she was solely referred to as the "spawn of the devil" by my aunt Hilda.

I've worked diligently to block out the memories of my time spent with my Aunt, her house full of Persian cats and her strict puritan beliefs. However, I will never forget the vacant look on my father's face as he drove off leaving me to fend for myself. That moment haunts me.

I watched as my father cursed the ground at my mother's funeral, swearing he would never love another woman.

Not long thereafter, with tears in his eyes, he amended his vow and said, "I will never love anyone ever again!"

Everybody at the funeral ignored his comment, but the weight of his words fell on me like a ton of bricks. I was stunned speechless.

Now I may be mistaken about what I am going to admit, but I swear my father was looking directly at me as he uttered those words. My childhood therapist tried to convince me otherwise. He said I "imagined it," but I distinctly recall my father's eyes changing. It was as if a light had shut off inside of him. From that day on I've been searching for true love.

Which subsequently leads me to the second time that I found myself dumbfounded and speechless. I was standing in front of a banner of the most romantic movie produced in the history of Hollywood when "she" strolled up and stood next to me.

The movie was *Lost in her Eyes*, starring Edie Greene and Jack Waters. It is and always will be my favorite movie. I was invited to a private screening of the re-release of the digitally enhanced film because I am, in fact, a well-known T.V. movie critic. While my television ratings are soaring, my fans are few. Most actors and filmmakers don't like what I have to say. They find me crude, overbearing and self-righteous. Truth be told... I am that way most of the time, but I haven't always been. Lately, I've been getting back to that time when I was hopeful and full of passion about life, love, and movies.

It all started when I looked over and saw HER. She was Edie Greene. Okay, she wasn't actually Edie Greene, but she certainly was a version of Edie Greene. My version, which in theory, meant that if she was Edie Greene, I could be Jack Waters. Jack Waters is a hero amongst swine, a man who just gets that four-letter word L-O-V-E right! So I turned to her and said, "Hello, I am Jack Waters and you must be Edie Greene?" She smiled and let out a small laugh of bewilderment. I responded in jest, "Don't tell me this is your first time seeing this movie?"

She remarked, "Are you kidding? I've seen this movie more times than I can count. This is and always will be my favorite movie!"

Now some might find it bizarre that this was the second moment that I was stunned to the point of speechlessness. But you see, from the moment I laid eyes on her I knew she was the woman I'd been waiting for my entire life. I stood there with my mouth agape as this fiery redhead described the best part of the movie to me.

She exclaimed, "My favorite part of *Lost in Her Eyes*, is when Edie realizes that she is madly in love with Jack Waters, whom, as you know, is about to go on a date with her dear friend. When Edie realizes what she's done, she totally freaks out and attempts to cancel her friend's date, but her friend is already under Jack's spell! To add insult to injury, her friend shows up at Jack's nightclub ready to seduce Jack wearing a hot little number that Edie picked out for her!" At that moment she turned towards me and sighed. "I felt so connected to Edie right at that instant. Can you imagine? What could be worse than that?"

As I stood there with my mouth agape, undoubtedly looking like a complete fool, I thought, this second? She went on for what seemed like an eternity and I said nothing. Before I could regain my composure, a group of her friends surrounded her like a swarm of honeybees and buzzed off. I tried to overcome the trance I was in, but it was too late. She was gone even before I asked her name.

She did however, turn around long enough to wave goodbye and call out, "It was nice to meet you Jack Waters!"

I tried to reciprocate with some sort of witty refrain; I called after her, "Till we meet again, Edie. Till' we meet again!"

That was three months ago today ...

MY LIFE IS UNFOLDING

Chapter One

No one seems to understand my dilemma. Ever since the day I met her, my life has been falling apart right in front of my eyes. I am engulfed in a deluge of memories, both good and bad.

At first, it was only at night. I'd wake up shivering in a cold sweat; feeling like a worm had just tunneled it's way through every quadrant of my brain, awakening memories I never knew existed. Then this nothingness burrowed its' way into my every waking hour. I would be getting ready for work and burst out into a fit of tears for no apparent reason. I kept thinking... it's got to be a phase? I tried meditating, going to the gym, sleeping in, I even gave tofu a try. Nothing worked!

In short, I was going out of my mind! Then the hallucinations and apparitions started. I began seeing her walking down the street and of course I started following her. Eventually one day I followed her into a café trying not to appear as creepy as I felt. I ordered a black cup of coffee and tapped her on the shoulder, not having a clue what I should say to her should she succumb to my wishes and turn around. She turned and looked over her shoulder at me, but she was no longer my Edie Greene, she had transformed into my late aunt Hilda! I dropped my cup of coffee and let out a loud scream darting out of the café. I scurried back to my apartment and hid under the covers like I had when I was a ten-years old. Only this time it wasn't the loss of my mother I was trying to cope with. This was much worse. I was seeing things. I pondered. Could I have imagined her all along? Could this woman whom I had briefly met have changed my life and be nothing more than a figment of my desperate imagination? An optical delusion?

That afternoon I went in to see my therapist Dr. Bloom and asked him if he would prescribe something for my "neurotic psychosis." In his very loud droning Jewish accent Dr. Bloom tried to console me.

"Charlie, none of it matters: the past, the present, or the future, if you can't find a way to be happy with the person you are."

I replied, "What if you don't know who you are?"

"Nonsense!" he said. "You are a successful movie critic Charlie. People from all around the world tune into watch your reviews even though without fail you trash every one of the movies you review. You have a big house, a fancy car, a yacht, and I'm assuming from the rates you pay me, a very healthy bank account. Look Charlie, you are not the type of person who should be spending his free time in therapy or chasing imaginary tail. And yet, you are. And you want to know why you are?"

I paused, I wasn't really sure I did want to know?

My therapist snorted. "I'll tell you why Charlie. It's simple… you like to suffer! You are here because you haven't learned how to let go. You cling to those negative memories of yours like they are your uniform just so you can keep digging them up at a later date and re-visit them all over again."

I scoffed. "That's not true!"

"Oh yes it is," he replied. "So why don't you just do us all a favor and give up this old routine of yours?"

"Okay," I said. Although I wasn't really sure what he was referring too? So I asked him, "How do you suppose I go about doing that?"

"It's simple Charlie, I want you to go home and start rummaging through some old photo albums. Your past shit, excuse me, I mean your buried memories can't hurt you Charlie when you simply learn to let them go. Now once you've finished going down memory lane why don't you pop a bag of jiffy pop and watch that movie you talked so much about. What's the name of it?"

"*Lost in Her Eyes,*" I responded.

"Yes, that's the one, re-visit it…. in fact re-visit every movie you've ever loved until you remember what it feels like to be happy again. As my Rabbi likes to say, "Success is not always the key to happiness, but happiness is the key to Success!" Dr. Bloom smiled and then yawned as he looked down at his watch and rubbed the top of it. "Well, unfortunately it looks like our time is up here Charlie, but I feel confident that our new therapy strategy will resolve some of your underlying issues."

"That's it!" I scoffed. "I came to you hallucinating and you want me to go home and rummage through old photo albums and watch movies?"

My therapist stood up. "That's right Charlie. I see a breakthrough coming your way. In fact, I am so sure of it that I'm going to go ahead and pencil you in for next week at this same time and let you come back and tell me how much my therapy has helped you."

Holy bonanzas! I thought to myself. He's lost his mind! For the first time in six years I left Dr. Bloom's office thinking this guy is a bigger bamboozler quack job than I am! How in the hell could watching old movies and looking at photo albums of my childhood, which I hated, help me? Needless to say, when I arrived home and started to walk down memory lane I was rather annoyed.

After mulling over the matter, I finally capitulated to Dr. Bloom's advice and set up the projector, which already had some old family slides loaded in the projector tray. The hot white light illuminated the blank white screen as I turned the machine on. I sat down and tried to advance the first slide, but it was jammed. "What the hell is the problem now?" I mumbled "Can't just one thing go right today?" I fiddled with the projector while puffing on an expensive Cuban cigar given to me by some dreadful filmmaker who had hoped his kind gesture might alter my normal scorching review, although he was sadly mistaken. Plumes of smoke filled the room clouding the image of me as an awkward looking newborn in a crib. I waved the smoke out of my face as I stared at the nostalgic image of myself projected on the wall. It was an aging photo of me sitting on a brand new red tricycle with my mother Evelyn standing proudly beside me. I sighed aloud and mumbled to myself in a sarcastic self-loathing tone. "Look at me all fresh and new ready for endless possibilities! Full of promise!" I clicked on the projector and a new image of me appeared on the screen as a goofy looking toddler clutching onto my mother's hand. "Okay, a little less promise here... cut the cord already kid!" I clicked again, and a slightly older version of myself appeared on the screen. I was sitting on the sofa next to my father, painfully crying at the top of my lungs, while my father ignored me. "Ah, quality time with dear old dad." I clicked the projector, annoyed by my lack of catharsis. Another image of me appeared, dressed in all black standing at my mother's funeral. "Now there is a family moment." I growled and quickly removed the slide from the projector tray and then clicked one last time. An awkward image of me standing in my college dorm room appeared on the wall. I looked like a total social outcast wearing a tattered and dirty t-shirt beneath a tweed sports coat. I tried to force a smile, "Keep trying kid! Keep trying and one day you'll be a swan amongst swine." I shut off the projector. "That's it!"

I pulled a copy of the film, *Lost in Her Eyes* off the shelf and popped it into my DVD player. Minutes later, I was sucked into the film and shoving handfuls of popcorn into my mouth. The T.V. screen displayed Jack Waters and Edie Greene. I stared at Jack Waters leaning on the bar flirting with Edie, a singer in his nightclub whom he had a long time secret crush on. Since it was after normal club hours they were the only two people left at the bar. Jack slid a drink towards Edie and they both lifted up their glasses. "Salute!"

The T.V. screen faded to black and then faded back in, indicating a passing of time. Jack and Edie appeared friendlier; they were sitting beside one another deep in conversation.

Jack smirked. "Edie do you really believe that true love exists?" Edie looked at Jack stunned. She grabbed her clutch off the bar and tapped Jack on the shoulder with it.

"Jack Waters! What kind of silly question is that?"

Jack laughed, "It's the kind of question that leads me to believe you do?"

Edie sipped her vodka martini. "Yes! Of course I do. Why? Don't you?"

Jack paused, and then coolly replied, "I don't know Edie. I have no proof of its existence."

Edie turned away, avoiding eye contact with Jack.

Jack helplessly stared at the back of Edie's head, willing her to turn around. Finally, he blurted out, "Well at least hear me out before you go and make any harsh judgments about me!"

Edie turned towards Jack and softly spoke. "Fine, I'm listening."

Jack took a sip of his bourbon and then cleared his throat. "What I was about to say was… couldn't it all be some chemical reaction going off in the brain?" Jack made a few hand gestures around his head indicating that sparks were going off.

Edie's face wrinkled in disgust. "How awful! Are you actually telling me Jack Waters doesn't believe in love?"

Jack stood up trying to play it cool. "I'm telling you that I'm not sure Edie. I don't think that I've ever been in love."

Edie's eyes softened as she tenderly caressed Jack's cheek. "How sad."

Jack grinned and leaned in playfully. "For whom?"

Edie rolled her eyes. "Very funny Jack."

Jack finished his drink and casually strolled behind the bar to pour another round. He arrogantly announced, "Yes, well I thought it was kind of clever."

Edie batted her long eyelashes at Jack and sighed, "Oh Jack! Poor misguided Jack. What are we going to do with you?"

Before Jack could reply Edie jumped off of her chair and screamed. "That's it!"

Jack nearly spit out his drink. "What? What did I miss?"

Edie stared intensely into Jack's eyes. "This summer, Jack Waters is going to fall in love!"

Jack choked on his words. "I am?"

Edie smiled and announced, "Yes, you are, because I am going to make it my personal mission to find that one incredible, irreplaceable woman that you can't live with out. You'll see; you won't be able to resist!"

Jack hated the idea, but he decided to play along with Edie's ridiculous plan just to see where it would go. "And just how might I ask do you plan on doing that?"

Edie twirled her red locks between her manicured fingers and sweetly cooed into Jack's ear. "Let's just say when it comes to matters of the heart, I am the love doctor."

Jack shook his head. "I see," he said, "but what if I refuse?"

Edie looked deep into Jack's eyes and whispered. "You can't resist a challenge Jack. Besides, what do you have to lose?"

Jack didn't skip a beat, "Everything!"

Edie leaned in closer and seductively replied, "Or you could gain everything Jack."

At that moment it was obvious that Jack would yield to Edie's every desire. "What do I have to do?"

Edie playfully clapped her hands and bit her bottom lip. "It's simple. You just have to go out to dinner with the women I set you up with and then… you have to let me help you woo them."

Jack looked at Edie like she was crazy. "What? Are you out of your mind? Why would I ever do a thing like that?"

Edie looked annoyed. "Why wouldn't you Jack? Unless you think I don't know what women want?" Jack didn't say a word. He knew he was on a slippery slope with Edie and he didn't want to mess up his chances with her.

"Well?" Edie said, anxiously anticipating Jack's response.

Jack smiled while shaking his head. "I don't know Edie. On the one hand, putting my love life in your hands could be the worst mistake of my life, but on the other hand you could have a point. You are a woman after all so; I suppose it is possible that you do know what women want."

Edie's face beamed with joy. "So you'll do it!"

Jack shook his head. "I didn't say that."

Edie's smile suddenly turned into a frown. "Fine then, I have to go!" Edie snatched her clutch off the bar and began to walk towards the door. "Goodnight Jack!"

Jack popped out from behind the bar and blocked Edie from leaving. "Hold on a minute. I'll do it, but only under one condition."

Edie squinted her eyes. "And what might that be?"

Jack grabbed Edie's hand. "One of those women has to be you."

Edie tapped Jack with her clutch again. "Jack that is ridiculous. And besides it defeats the whole purpose of this."

Jack took a deep breath and said, "You are either one of the women Edie or we don't have a deal."

Edie tried to argue with Jack, but he cut her off with a hard glance. "Fine! I'll be one of the women, but nothing is going to happen between the two of us Jack so you better make the most of the women I set you up with."

Jack moved out of Edie's way. "We'll see about that, won't we?" Edie rolled her eyes and then walked out of the bar.

Unexpectedly, the sound from the T.V. set was replaced with the sound of my snoring. I had passed out on the couch with my hand in the popcorn bowl.

THE DARK CAVERNS OF MY MIND

Chapter Two

The next morning I woke up in a cold sweat. My nightmares were getting worse. I felt like a car ran me over in the middle of the night. I was troubled by the thought of never seeing this woman again. I popped a few anti-anxiety pills hoping to dull my senses, but it was useless.

That afternoon I drove to work expecting the worst. I day dreamed my "imaginary female friend" the fiery redhead that had been haunting my very existence would hop into my car while I was stopped at the traffic light, seduce me and suggest that we drive off into the sunset together. Of course I would agree to it, mesmerized by her every move, realizing only after I'd arrived in Mexico that I was having yet, another hallucination!

This time of course, my delightful delusion would not be of my dead aunt Hilda, but rather a young male prostitute whose testicles had yet to drop. I sighed at the thought of being fooled in such a humiliating fashion. I tried to clear my mind of these irrational thoughts by turning on the radio, but it was hopeless. The dark caverns of my mind were under siege by this woman and when I arrived at the television studio I was ready to snap heads.

Walking through the labyrinth of lights, the staff timidly stared at me as I entered their space, but continued to scurry to and fro making preparations for the taping of my show *Angry Movie Guy*, hosted by yours truly, Charlie Evans correction by yours truly, Charlie "The Snake" Evans.

I felt worse than I had in months as I entered my dressing room in a rage and changed into my on-camera attire: a well-tailored blue Armani suit with thin white pin stripes. I moaned aloud as I stared at my reflection in the mirror. I tried to suck in my paunch. "Suck it in you troll!" I was disgusted with myself. I'd outgrown my third suit in six months. I took a deep breath and buttoned my suit and opened the door of my dressing room. I saw my staff progressing toward me and I immediately shut the door. My heart was palpitating. Would I have another hallucination on-camera while I tried to give today's review? No, I thought, mentally trying to pull myself up by the bootstraps with an egomaniacal pep talk. "I am Charlie f'n "The Snake" Evans. Movie critic! Thousands of people tune in to watch my review every week. I am not the type of person who hallucinates. I am not the type of person who spends his spare time at the therapist office. I have a yacht for Christ sakes!" Opening the door, I walked out to the middle of the set. Standing motionless, like a statue with my head bowed and my eyes closed I fished through my jacket pocket for my bottle of therapy and poured a few pills into my mouth and swallowed hard.

I could hear the voice of the stage manager off camera. "You ready Charlie?"

Without opening my eyes I sat down in a dark brown plush leather chair on-set and elegantly crossed my legs nodding to the stage manager as I swiveled my chair to face the camera.

The cameraman peered at me with a cold and vacant look, as the director yelled, "And Action!"

I stared into the camera for an uncomfortable amount of time before flashing a sardonic smile. I watched as the crew gathered around the monitors to view another hideous taping of my show and I muttered, "Why me?"

I eyed Samantha, my wiry blonde personal assistant, whom I imagine deeply despises my existence standing close by observing the close-up of me on the monitor. I reached for the remote control to turn on the television set, a clip from *The Hunt for a New World.... Master of the Far Seas* appeared on the screen. The monitor displayed a weathered captain on the deck of a sailing ship staring out into the abyss of the Pacific through a telescope.

I began to speak with a concerned, almost fatherly tone of voice using long dramatic pauses for effect. "Good evening, my fellow moviegoers, tonight I'm going to try something a little different, tonight I am going to pray. I encourage all of you at home to do the same."

Out of the corner of my eye, I watched as Samantha stared down at the script in disgust, the same way she stares at me when she thinks I'm not looking.

I bent down on both knees. "Dear Lord, with your infinite wisdom and compassion, I'm confused as to how you could let the *Hunt for a New World... Master of the Far Seas* ever be put to film?

Lord? Why? Why, when women and children are dying of famine and neglect throughout your glorious Kingdom would you ever let the director spend one hundred and thirty-five million dollars to manufacture cinematic toilet paper trash? Crackers! I should have gotten the clue when I read the pretentious title. Crackers! And you call yourself God? Well let me tell you something, this never-ending 17th century naval misadventure made me feel like I had been through Genesis and Revelation. I mean look...."

My assistant Samantha let out a loud yelp as I shot up from the floor and flashed a menacing glare at the camera. I scowled in her direction and she quickly covered her mouth and ducked behind the monitors ferociously writing in her logbook.

Meanwhile, the camera had panned to the video feed to show the captain in the movie staring out into the abyss. I dropped to my knees, yet again and began to speak in an evangelical tone.

"Look!" I continued, "He is still peering through his telescope, which he no doubt needs to compensate for his tiny..."

I winked into the camera as I held up my pinky finger, wiggling it to indicate that the captain has a small dingy.

Annoyed by my ostentatiousness, I observed Samantha cringe as she watched me pace to and fro cackling with egotistical condescension. I began to imagine what meaningless nonsense she must be scribbling into her logbook and I began to stutter. I grabbed the remote control from off the floor. "Now..now wa..wa..watch this."

I heard the director yell to the cameraman. "Lets get a close up on this!"

He motioned for the cameraman to zoom in on me as I fast-forwarded the movie so the audience could see that the captain was still standing in the exact same position with another crewmember.

I smirked. "Been on that ship together a bit too long have ya?"

Trying not to be bothered by my obnoxious assistant I continued with my rant. I threw the remote control into the air flailing my hands wildly as I bellowed, "Sure, sure, it's historically conscientious, but come on! The ice caps are melting faster than this movie and are more entertaining to watch. You're stuck on a boat. How many stoic glances can you give to your shipmates anyway before they throw you overboard?"

Samantha began to giggle as she watched me begin to lose my composure. My turmoil was amusing her and all those who surrounded the monitors. I began to stammer as I continued to rant. I exclaimed, "Look, most of the film is spent building all this dramatic tension, and for what? To attack the pansy beret wearing Frenchies! Crackers!"

I stood up shaking my fists at the ceiling as though admonishing God. The crewmembers looked on nervously as I screamed and then lowered myself into my chair like an exhausted father who has just used up all his energy scolding a child. Staring into the camera with an expression of hopeless regret I muttered, "Like our hot headed leading man, I have a duty to fulfill and that duty is to impart some wisdom to the less than esteemed director. The next time you're making a movie be sure it has a script!"

I saw Samantha look over at the crew who now seemed relieved thinking that my tirade was over until it became clear that I was not yet exhausted.

I pointed my finger at the camera unwillingly to compromise my review. "I bet you think you're real funny getting a theater full of people to pay $14.00 just to sit there with their thumbs up their butts, bored out of their skulls because they're waiting for a ship that will never sink in a battle, in a war that will never happen! Crackers!" By now my blood was boiling and my eyes were bloodshot as I drove my point home. "Twenty books to work from and this is the best that you could do? Well let me tell you, that neither the general public, nor I will be so stupid as to get sucked into your egotistical narcissistic self-indulgence! I give this pathetic excuse of a film two thumbs down and the middle finger."

I glared into the camera and stuck my two thumbs down and my middle finger out simultaneously vindicating all the moviegoers who wasted their time and money on a piece of garbage.

Just then I looked up and saw a newbie at the studio patting Samantha on the back, assuring her my tirade was almost over. I wanted to scream, but instead I addressed the camera with civil composure. "Thank you and until next time, don't tread on Charlie "The Snake" Evans."

I watched as Samantha looked over at the director who was yelling, "And we're out!"

Lying back in my chair I watched in agitated dismay as my assistant Samantha giggled at me rather than coming to my aid. I was no longer slick and in control. I immediately began to have a sneezing fit. I tried to move from my chair, but my microphone was tangled. I kicked the chair and mumbled to myself in between sneezes.

Samantha and the newbie stared at me, amused by the fiasco until the director motioned for Sam to check on me.

"Fine!" She mumbled.

Sam set her clipboard down and rushed to my side to untangle my microphone.

I sat up. "Samantha, I know jumping at every opportunity to fulfill the minutest need of mine completes you as a human being..."

Samantha dropped the tangled cord, dumbfounded by my comment. "No, Mr. Evans... It's just..."

I held up my finger interrupting her. "Ahh! Ahh! Shh, shh, shh.... please don't waste the sad fact that your parents once had sex and all of those glorious cells divided to one day create you!"

Samantha blinked her eyes in silence. She seemed afraid. She looked around and saw the entire crew staring at her as I laughed in her face. "I'm sorry. What I meant to say is get a damn life!" Samantha reeled backwards in horror and ran off the set in tears.

The crewmembers scattered as I bolted toward my dressing room, red-faced from anger, sneezing all the way there. "Damn it! Damn it! Damn it!" Entering my dressing room I lunged for the bathroom to puke, revealing the wall of hate mail from outraged filmmakers and actors of films that I'd reviewed.

I stared at my reflection in the mirror. I looked gaunt and haggard. It was a huge contrast to what I was on set just moments earlier. Leaning on the dressing room table I inspected myself, wiping my face with a towel and shaking my head in disgust. I tapped on the mirror. "You are such a waste Charlie." I flipped myself the bird and then closed my eyes and slumped down into a luxurious leather chair, passing out exhausted from life. I began dreaming of a time when things were… well to be honest, things were not too much better than they are now, but at least they were over.

In a dreamy, blurry haze I traveled back in time to my college graduation. I was last in a dwindling lineup of graduates. The audience was clapping vigorously for a new college graduate who was beaming as she walked off the stage holding up her diploma. The applause died down and the female master of ceremonies leaned in to speak.

"Last, but certainly not least, Charlie…" *Squalkkk*! The microphone squeaked loudly, which made my name inaudible. The audience members muttered their displeasure as the microphone feedback slowly deteriorated.

"Okay, quiet down. Quiet down, please! Last, but certainly not least, Charlie Zimmerman!"

The MC at the podium was the only one who enthusiastically clapped in a sea of silence. The audience began laughing and groaning as I walked to the middle of the stage and stopped dead in my tracks.

The college kids in my dream began to harass me. "What the hell is this dufus doing?"

Another college kid chimed in, "Who knows, he's such a fucking weirdo."

I began to toss in my sleep and then suddenly, without warning, in my dream I saw my astral-self fly out of my body on stage and levitate over me in the auditorium. I couldn't believe my eyes. I was having such a vivid dream.

Astral Charlie, in his etheric body screamed, "Whoo! Hoo! Look at me. I'm free! Free as a bird!" He began to laugh as he looked down at me, frozen in the middle of the stage like a moron until he noticed something strange. "Hey, that guy kind of looks like me." Astral Charlie flew down and looked into my eyes. "Man the likeness is uncanny, but I bet that guy can't fly like me." Astral Charlie flew back up to the ceiling and did the backstroke in mid air. He looked down at the crowd of people who were now screaming and throwing their graduation caps at me as I just stood there in the middle of the stage looking like a melting ice sculpture. Sweat dripped down the side of my face. I watched as my astral self swooped down and sort of patted my head dry. Astral Charlie screamed out, "Someone turn on the air conditioning!" He looked around at the audience. "Uh oh, these college students seem to be getting angry."

A disgruntled college kid yelled out, "Get off the stage dork!"

Another punk from the audience yelled, "There's a party to go to asshole!"

And yet another college graduate piped up. "Come on Dimmerman let's wrap it up!"

Astral Charlie nervously watched as I stood on the stage clenching my fists while being hit by flying graduation caps. "This look-a-like is giving me a bad name. Come on buddy! There's nothing to be afraid of here. It's just a bunch of people who don't even know you. Not the real you, so they can't begin to judge you, right?"

Just then a cute girl called out from the audience. "Yeah Dimmerman! Have a wet dream on your own time!" The whole audience laughed.

Astral Charlie looked at the girl shocked. "Okay, well maybe she knows you but, still… we're beginning to look a little weird up here so why don't you just do us both a favor and move it along." Astral Charlie froze in mid air realizing what he had just said. He grabbed his face and then his body. "Wait a second! I'm you? I mean…you're me? Oh! This is all too much for me to deal with. I need a drink." Astral Charlie's voice echoed in my head as I peered further into the dream.

I saw Dean Rutherford; a smooth dark skinned young black man walking towards me in a crème double-breasted suit. He leaned in and whispered into my ear. "Are you alright, son?" Scared stiff, I peered sideways towards the young black man and shook my head no. The man looked out at the disgruntled audience and whispered in my ear. "Just remember what I said: they all love you." I suppose that I was searching for the right words to say, but nothing I thought of seemed to match the moment so instead I said nothing.

Astral Charlie looked desperate. He moaned, "He won't listen to you. He doesn't listen to reason. Oh for crying out loud Charlie! Move!" Astral Charlie looked out into the audience and saw my father arriving. He was walking into the auditorium several hours late. Astral Charlie yelled, "Asshole!" My father strutted down the aisle with a dark haired long legged woman on his arm that was decked from head to toe in Chanel. Astral Charlie glared at them as they made their way to their seats.

I felt cheated even in my dream as I watched Yasmine, my father's raven-haired girlfriend squeeze into an empty seat. She entered my father's life at a time when he decided that although he may never love another woman he would certainly fuck again!

I could see my father squinting and pointing at me as I stood in the middle of the stage. "That's Charlie there," he whispered in Yasmine's ear. "I had hoped the first time you met my kid he wouldn't be embarrassing himself, but I can see that was too much to ask for."

As I looked out into the audience from the stage I saw my father sit down and I began to walk towards the podium. The audience began to clap as I moved to receive my diploma. Watching myself in my dream, it seemed like I had been waiting for my father to show up all along. The minute I saw my father I unclenched my fist and dropped the object that I had been holding. It didn't make sense to me. Why would I be carrying a picture of my mother to my graduation only to drop it when my deadbeat father arrived?

I walked up to the podium and Dean Rutherford grabbed my hand and shook it so hard that I thought it would fall off. He turned to the audience beaming. "Can I get your attention?" The crowd ignored him. "Can I get your attention please?" I was hopelessly standing next to Mr. Rutherford wishing for a quick death. "Can I get your attention now!" The crowd quieted. "Thank you! As I was saying, every year we award one graduating student for their outstanding achievements and this year is no exception. It is with great pleasure that I announce the winner and let me tell you this kid is one of a kind!"

I felt violated as I watched this surreal dream unfolding before my eyes. There was Ray, my quote unquote "father" snuggling up to his girlfriend Yasmine as if they were in a drive in theater. He cooed into her ear, "Yeah, he is a one of a kind fuck-up!" Yasmine laughed and squeezed Ray's arm. The audience continued to snicker at me.

Astral Charlie floated above me. "Let's hurry this up. I want to get this side show act over Charlie!"

Dean Rutherford began to engage the audience. "Charlie Zimmerman, on behalf of the entire faculty I'd like to congratulate you and present you with this years most prestigious award, the Kensington University Award for Outstanding Achievement." There was sparse, unenthusiastic clapping coming from the audience. I looked stupefied as Dean Rutherford handed me a plaque. "We sure are going to miss you son. Go on, say something." The Dean pushed me towards the microphone. I tried to fake a smile, but I saw my father laughing and Yasmine giggling.

Astral Charlie looked at Ray and then at me. "Come on Charlie, ignore him. This is your day. You can always look back on this day and be proud of yourself. You earned this buddy!"

Looking out into the audience I leaned into the microphone as I held up my plaque and mustered up the only word I could think of. "Thanks."

I turned around and rushed off the stage hoping that I would never have to see any of my classmates again. This was not going to be difficult since none of them actually liked me and I was planning to move to Siberia.

The faculty presenter returned to the podium and gave an announcement. "One last thing… congratulations! Remember the future is yours!"

I could hear the audience cheering as I walked off the stage. The students began to disperse and it grew dark. The darkness was eerie. I thought to myself, "Thank God, this awful dream is coming to an end!" Until, it became clear that this was not the case.

Rolling over in my sleep, I woke up somewhere else in the dream world. Behind me, I saw a lamp sitting on an end table. Clicking on the lamp I saw my therapist Dr. Bloom standing in what appeared to be a long corridor.

"What are you doing here Dr. Bloom?"

Dr. Bloom put his arm around me. "Don't worry Charlie, this session is on me. We are going to crack this neurosis of yours if it's the last thing we do."

I thought of running, but a woman with slicked back hair wearing a white lab coat came out of nowhere and grabbed me by the arm and began walking me down the corridor. On the walls of the corridor were pictures of me that I didn't remember taking. The woman in the lab coat handed me a few pills and said in a thick Russian accent. "Here, take these. It will ease the pain Charlie."

I grabbed the pills and swallowed hard as I stared at the photos. It was as if someone had been following me with a hidden camera my entire life taking pictures of the worst possible moments and then had decided to frame them. Studying a picture of myself I remarked, "The only thing nice about this picture is the frame." Shaking my head, I tried hard not to look. When I got to the end of the corridor I hit a door marked, **DO NOT ENTER**, written in bold letters. "What should I do?" I said, as I turned to the woman in the white lab coat, but she vanished like a ghost and the walls surrounding me were now beginning to cave in. I began to panic. I yanked the door open and ran inside shutting the door in the brink of time. I leaned against the door taking several deep breaths before opening my eyes to see what I had gotten myself into. The room was glowing blue.

As I walked further inside I saw another version of myself sitting at a table chain smoking surrounded by purring Persian cats. The woman in the white lab coat materialized again as I began to hyperventilate.

She handed me a bag. "Here!"

"This is a dream. I'm dreaming, aren't I?" I said as I gasped for air.

"I need to wake up! Can you give me something to WAKE UP?"

The woman in the coat shook her head, indifferent to my pain. I was convulsing in fear as I looked into the eyes of my double that was chain smoking. I screamed, "You won't take me alive!" Then I hysterically rammed myself into the wall thinking that this would end the hallucinogenic dream sequence I was having. I waited.

Moments later, Astral Charlie released himself from my unconscious body. There were now three versions of myself in my dream. I watched as Astral Charlie soared around the room. "Ahhh! Much better! I feel a lot better out here Charlie. Charlie!?" Astral Charlie looked below him and saw that I was lying on the ground.

The woman in the lab coat looked up at Astral Charlie and said in her thick Russian accent. "Charlie is unavailable at the moment."

Astral Charlie shook his head, "Oh great! It's just like you to collapse when things are getting a little hairy. You know what… forget it. I'll check it out myself." Still lingering in the air, Astral Charlie shouted at my still body lying in the middle of the floor. "So this Charlie double of your is up to something. I'll take a closer look." Astral Charlie flew to the second Charlie and peered over his shoulder. "He's job hunting Charlie! Ugh! Just forget about it. They don't want you! I know your heart is set on being a movie critic, but if you knew what I know you wouldn't even bother picking up that phone." My double picked up the phone and was about to dial when a look of hopelessness came over him. He hung up the phone in despair and flung himself down on the sofa just missing one of the Persian cats. Astral Charlie smiled. "That a boy Charlie. It's for the best, believe me, you'll be thanking me for this one day." My double tossed and fidgeted for a bit before he seemed to drift off into a blissful depressed induced sleep. Astral Charlie sighed as he flew back over to where I was lying on the floor unconscious. "Well I think I convinced your double to throw in the towel. No need to thank me now. You can always take me out for dinner later. My favorite is Thai by the way. I know you don't like it, but you'll take one for the team this time, won't ya?" Astral Charlie smirked and then groaned, "Damn! Today already Charlie! This woman in the smock is giving me the creeps. Did you notice she has a mustache? Charlie?" Astral Charlie turned towards the woman in the white coat and smiled at her as he watched her push a red button on the wall.

My head felt like it was going to explode as I observed the room begin to rumble and spin in my dream. I began to feel nauseous. The woman glared at Astral Charlie as she watched him try to grab onto the walls. Astral Charlie whimpered. "What's happening? The room is spinning out of control Charlie. Save me!" Finally, the room began to settle and Astral Charlie opened his eyes and looked around him. He stared in awe. "It's our old apartment Charlie!" All of a sudden, the apartment began to split apart to reveal it as nothing more than a television set. "Whoa! Would you look at that?" Astral Charlie tried to wake up both

Charlie's in my dream, but the woman in the coat stopped him. Consequently, stopping me from waking up from my dream.

"Let the poor boy sleep," she said.

Astral Charlie decided it was up to him to explore the new headquarters. With the walls of the apartment gone Astral Charlie could see the soundstage in the distance, a lone VTR monitor was blinking. He flew in to get a closer look. "Hey Charlie! There is a monitor here."

The VTR monitor flickered on what appeared to be Tex Meed, an American film critic and former co-host of the syndicated television show, *We is Gone to the Movies*. Tex was sitting in front of what appeared to be the cast from *Star Wars* who were all eating a cake that was in the shape of my head! Astral Charlie grinned. "Nice!" Astral Charlie looked back at my double sleeping soundly on the couch and then at me still lying passed out on the floor. "You're missing the show Charlie." Astral Charlie flew back over and stared down at my crooked body. "Are you going to just lay there like a lump on a log?" The room fell silent. "Fine, if it has to be this way then so be it." Astral Charlie reluctantly re-entered my lifeless body lying on the floor like he was being sucked into a vacuum.

I watched myself wake up in my dream and rub the bump that had swelled up on the back of my head. My dream appeared blurry as this new part of my consciousness tried to associate with its surroundings. By now my other self had completely given up from job hunting and was passed out on the couch and Tex Meed was live on the VTR Monitor.

Tex addressed the screen in his standard fashion. "Doing what I do, you come across more than one pathetic character, it's much like a Star Wars convention, but Charlie Zimmerman takes the cake. A sorrier soul there has never been and if you can find one I will take you out to dinner myself."

Chubaka let out a wail and threw a piece of cake at Tex Meed. The screen flickered to show Dean Malit, the American film and book critic.

Dean Malit leaned into the camera. "I was astounded when I found out just what a putz Charlie Zimmerman... I mean Charlie Evan's truly is. He gets walked on by quadriplegics! If failure were gold, this kid would have the Midas Touch."

The screen changed again to *The NitPicker* an animated T.V. show that revolves around the life of the film critic, Ray Lerman. The animated character Ray Lerman smirked into the camera. "Hello people! I'm here to talk about Charlie Evan's, a man who makes yours truly look like Warren Beatty. Yowza! There are but two words in the English vocabulary to describe Mr. Evan's: He Stinks!"

The screen went black and for a second I thought the humiliating jam session was over, but then the lights came up behind me. I turned to see Dr. Bloom standing there with a dress coat in his hands.

"Here put this on Charlie."

We both took a seat near the front of the stage that had appeared in my dream. There seemed to be some type of award show going on, with an opulent stage, like the Oscars, and a lavish set. Turning around I saw gorgeous audience members filling the seats behind me. Carl Jung, the Swiss psychiatrist and founder of analytical psychology and Sigmund Freud, the Austrian neurologist and founding Father of psychoanalysis stood behind the podium in the center of the stage.

Jung held an envelope in his hands. "This is exciting!"

Freud looked at Jung. "Jung, your hands are shaking."

Jung's eyes widened with excitement. "I know it's all the pressure, Freud." Jung ripped open the seal to the envelope and read aloud. "And the best loser for outstanding life underachievement award goes to… Charlie Zimmerman!" Freud and Jung applauded and the audience followed throughout the auditorium.

I yelled out from the audience. "Oh come on!" I looked around at the audience members for help. "Is that really necessary?" Everyone ignored me, except for a fourth Charlie dressed in a tacky pale blue tuxedo sitting behind me. The fourth Charlie leaned forward and told me to, "Zip it," as he bounded awkwardly up the steps to the stage and took his award. Freud and Jung both shook his hand.

I looked at Dr. Bloom and whispered, "What is this guy doing? Is he a moron?"

My trained psychiatrist looked at me and said, "I think what you mean to say is, are you a moron?" His words hit me like a ton of bricks and I jolted in my sleep. Just then a wall dropped out of the side of the room and Morey Spellman yelled, "Don't listen to him Charlie. Come sit next to me over here by the pool!"

"By the pool?" I exclaimed.

I turned and saw Morey Spellman waiving to the fourth Charlie with a huge smile across his face as he sipped on a Piña Colada in a pair of yellow swim trunks covered with Hawaiian girls in hula skirts. I watched as the fourth Charlie walked over in his tacky baby blue tux and sat on a dirty lounge chair next to Morey Spellman and picked up a Piña Colada and began to sip it. I observed in disbelief as a beautiful waitress walked up to him with a phone on a platter. The phone was ringing nonstop.

Morey nudged him. "Pick it up man! That's your future calling!"

He looked at the phone and then up at Morey. "You're Morey Spellman!"

Morey rolled his eyes and took a deep breath. "Yeah, I know, now pick up the phone." But he just sat there in his tacky baby blue tux staring at Morey Spellman.

"I loved you in *The Found Boys*.

Morey nodded his head. "Yeah, who didn't? Dude! Answer the PHONE!"

He looked at the phone again. "Oh yeah!" The fourth Charlie picked up the phone from the tray and spoke. "Hello?" He held the phone away from his ear. "That's weird." The phone was still ringing even though he had answered it.

I watched as the wind began to blow. It was blowing lightly at first, but then it picked up and began to blow so hard that both my look-a-like and Morey got up off their lounge chairs.

My look-a-like stared at Morey. "Man...the wind is really blowing!"

Morey rolled his eyes. "Yeah... no shit Sherlock; I think we should go inside." They both tried to walk towards the lingering audience, but the wind was blowing so hard that they were moving backwards. Meanwhile, the audience members were dispersing from the award show. They were disturbed by this new part of my consciousness that was un-folding.

Morey tried to take a sip of his drink, but it blew right out of his hand.

My look-a-like swallowed hard as he watched Morey's drink being whisked away. He exclaimed, "I think it's a typhoon!"

I tried to exit the award show with the other frantic audience members, but I was whisked from Dr. Bloom's side and landed right next to my look-a-like in the baby blue tux. We turned to one another and screamed. "A typhoon!"

My look a-like grabbed me by the shoulders. "What the hell is a typhoon doing in your dream?"

"I don't know!" I screamed.

Dr. Bloom and the woman in the white lab coat appeared beside Morey Spellman and they all shrieked, "Well, why the hell don't you wake up?" The phone began ringing again and I furiously awoke in my dressing room.

SELF REALIZATION

Chapter Three

I sprung up from the couch and grabbed my cell phone. "Hello?" The person on the other end began screaming.

"Where the hell are you Charlie? I've been trying to reach you all afternoon. Get your butt down here!"

Glancing at my watch, I realized I'd been asleep for almost two hours. I walked to the mirror and stared at my reflection. I looked fatigued. My appearance was so alarming that I forgot that I was on the phone, till I heard Harry scream at the top of his lungs.

"Charlie! What kind of stunt are you trying to pull now? Charlie!!!"

"Yeah, I'm here." I said, sounding groggy and depressed.

Harry barked at me. "I've been waiting to speak with you for over an hour. I'm here at La Mystique with two gorgeous women who are practically begging me to go home with them. So hurry the hell up!"

I feigned a cough. "I'm sorry, I'm not feeling that well Harry."

Harry snorted, "Yeah, right. I hope you're not coming down with the flu Charlie because I've got something serious I need to discuss with you."

I rolled my eyes as I continued to stare at my reflection in the mirror while listening to Harry rattle on and on. I realized Harry couldn't care less about what happened to me. As long as Harry was making money and the ratings on the show were going up, Harry was manageable. The minute the ratings dropped there would be hell to pay and that hell will come out of my, you know what! Luckily for me my ratings were skyrocketing otherwise this little stunt would have pushed Harry over the edge.

It seemed to me that the more irreverent I became the more people fell in love with hating me and tuned in to watch me. It was useless arguing with ratings, so I don't even know why I tried.

I blurted out, "I'm fine Harry. I'll be there in fifteen minutes!"

I hung up the phone and made my way to meet Harry. I jumped into my silver Porsche and drove down the highway like a bat out of hell mumbling to myself about being late. I knew the one thing Harry hated almost as much as losing ratings was when I was late. I sped up Park Avenue, cursing and honking at every slow person on the road. "Learn how to drive you old bag!" I screamed. The old bag flipped me the bird and merged in front of me and began to drive even slower than before. "Shit. I can't win."

I turned on the radio in hopes of calming my nerves, but of course, it was an ad for Viagra. I sighed aloud. I hadn't had sex with a woman in years. I liked to tell myself it was because I was afraid of all the diseases I could catch, but truthfully it was because I couldn't stand the sight of myself. Turning the dial on the receiver I found my favorite radio program. It was one of those programs where people called in to discuss their problems. They had a well-known male psychiatrist hosting the show named Dr. W. I liked the program because I felt relieved about my own situation when I had the opportunity to listen to how fucked up the rest of the world is. I listened with a smirk on my face as people balled their eyes out over their failed marriages, kids on drugs, callers who were in serious debt from student loans and families losing their homes to the bank. I suppose I also tuned in because I thought that Dr. W gave these poor souls inspiration to carry on in times of emotional and physical despair. I knew no matter how famous Harry tried to make me, I was one of those poor lost souls. I considered going to see Dr. W a couple of times, but I quickly changed my mind after my current therapist, Dr. Bloom assured me we were on the verge of a major break through. That was nearly three years ago.

    I pulled into a parking garage two blocks away from La Mystique. I would rather valet at La Mystique, but last time I did some young punk slashed my tires or maybe it was a disgruntled waiter. Either way, I regretted that Harry was a regular at La Mystique because it meant that I was a regular. The only up side to the occasion was that I knew Harry would pay and leave a very generous tip. It was for this reason that the waiters put up with my obnoxious behavior and rude insults. That and I am a "star" who is known for being over the top, downright insulting, and gregarious. While speed walking towards the restaurant I made a firm decision about my life. I would call Dr. W this week. I needed something to calm my nerves. I was utterly convinced that Dr. Bloom's movie therapy wasn't going to do the trick.

Walking into the restaurant I spotted Harry sitting between two blondes whilst sipping on a martini. For as long as I've known Harry, he has been a real pain in my ass. He is an honest to God character, that never goes unnoticed with his cowboy hat, flowery Desigual dress shirts and steeled-toed boots; he is a real Hollywood cowboy living in the heart of Manhattan. In other words, the man stands out like a sore thumb everywhere he goes, including La Mystique, the finest French restaurant in Manhattan. Harry is the exact opposite of me with his flashy clothes, arm candy, and the endless rounds of vodka martinis served to him with one green olive.

From the door I could see that one of the blondes was wearing his cowboy hat, while the other one rubbed his shiny baldhead as Harry gawked at her exposed cleavage.

A tall lanky flamboyantly gay waiter named Sean strutted up to the table and set another round of drinks down, at which point Harry noticed me. It was obvious that he had been eyeing the door since we hung up. I saw him try to excuse himself.

"Finally!"

I'm sure Harry wanted to berate me, but not in front of the woman he was trying to woo into his hot tub and later on into his bed for an all night session of fellatio. The two blondes with him looked like total plastic bimbos. I rolled my eyes at the mere sight of them and slowly walked towards the table. Harry attempted to excuse himself again.

"Excuse me." Harry said, as he struggled to remove himself from the booth yet again, but the women were oblivious to his intent and thus prevented him from going anywhere. I heard them babbling as I approached.

"What is it? Where are you going Harry?"

Harry pointed at me. "Charlie is here."

I approached the table with a look of exhaustion plastered across my face while Sean impatiently stood beside them with one hand on his hip waiting for the ladies to order. He turned when he saw me arrive and immediately blurted out.

"Oh, look who's arrived, if it isn't my favorite movie critic. I thought Mr. Happy-face was taking a day off from destroying his liver." Sean threw his head back in disgust and pranced away mumbling French curse words.

I snarled at him. He was lucky I wasn't feeling good. Normally, I would have attempted to trip him for making such a wise crack. Instead, I took my fowl mood out on Harry's plastic bimbos. I gave the most inappropriate greeting I could think of. "Harry." Harry nodded his head. "Concubines - err - ladies."

Sean returned with a drink and handed it to me. I downed it in one gulp and set the empty glass back onto Sean's tray. He shrugged his shoulder.

"Aw, it looks like our superstar has had himself a bad day."

"It's a bad decade actually. Now bring me another drink, and this time put some bourbon in it."

Sean glared at me and whispered loudly. "You are such an asshole!"

I shook my head. "Well, you are the expert here in that part of the anatomy."

Sean stormed off mumbling under his breath. "You wish you could get with this honey!"

Harry chuckled. "That's what I hired you for kid. You tell it like it is. There is no beating around the bush with you, Charlie. Now tell me, what's the matter with you? You look like shit."

The girls giggled. I glanced at them and then back at Harry. I leaned in and whispered into his ear.

"You better do something with them before I ruin your plans at having a ménage à trois."

Harry immediately snuggled up to the two women. "Ladies, why don't you do me a favor and go get yourself a drink at the bar." Both of the girls kissed Harry on either side of his face leaving red lipstick on his cheeks. One of the girls seductively dressed in a low cut Dior dress whispered into his ear.

"Sure Mr. Puebei, but don't take too long because we're anxious to get back to your place, un-pack, and take a dip in that Jacuzzi of yours." Harry blushed.

"Oooh wee! Now that's what I'm talking about. Okay, I'll make this fast!"

The blondes tried to excuse themselves from the table. "Excuse me."

I stared at them and crossed my legs to let them slip past, but before they could actually fully remove themselves from the booth I took the opportunity to insult them. I grabbed one of the blonde's French manicured hands and pummeled her with my remarks.

"Can I ask you a question?"

41

She looked at me like a deer in headlights. "Sure."

"Have you filed for capital gain credits on those?"

The two blondes looked at one another confused. "Capital what?"

I smirked, "Gains. For those." I pointed at each breast sticking out towards me, one at a time. "They must have cost, what... seven grand each? That could be quite a lifesaver come April 15th. I mean they are a work expense, right?"

Harry choked on his drink. The girls covered their exposed cleavage and looked towards Harry for help. Harry put his arm around me. "Truth be told it was closer to nine grand each, and worth every cent!" The girls smiled and hugged Harry, who enjoyed the attention. "Don't listen to him ladies. He's just jealous. Go get yourself a drink and I'll finish up with Charlie." Harry signaled to the bartender to get the ladies a round on him before turning his attention to me. He took a sip of his martini, unfazed by my comments.

Sean placed another bourbon in front of me as Harry continued, "Okay, now let's get down to business. You know I've been working on a deal to get this movie made about you?"

I nodded my head. "It's all your ego has been talking about for the past six months."

Harry put his arm around me. "Well sit back and relax because I've managed to get the interest of some real Hollywood bigwigs. But there's a catch..."

I looked up at the ceiling. "Isn't there always?"

Harry rubbed his hands together. "They say all you do is pan big budget Hollywood studio films."

I shrugged my shoulders. "What can I say, I like big targets."

Harry squeezed my shoulders. "That is the point my friend. They say it's time to pick on the little guy. Here is your pass to the second annual New York *Film Frenzy Indie Film Festival*. The festival began as a tribute to Fellini." Harry slid an envelope towards me. I opened it and took out a ticket and a laminated tag.

I stared at it, *Four Golden Stars,* by Alex Rasner. "Who the hell is he?" I snarled.

Harry laughed. "Who knows and who cares? Probably some indie film maker who just got distribution for his first film and will probably drop off the face of the planet. Listen Charlie, they want you to liven it up a little and see you go after an artist or something. This is the perfect film for you to review. I hear there are whales mating in it."

I scooped up the nametag and ticket and pocketed it. "Enough said. I'll prove myself to be an equal opportunity asshole and go to this flick. See you later. Those bimbos of yours are giving me a headache."

Harry slapped me on the back. "Fantastic! Later amigo! And I want you to know we've got them. You are going to have a movie made about you in no time."

I headed towards the door. "That's fantastic Harry, I'm really looking forward to having two hours of my pathetic life being broadcasted all across America!"

Harry screamed. "What are you talking about? We are going to make you an international star! Don't worry Charlie. I know what I'm doing. Stick with me and there will be a little *Angry Movie Guy* bobble-head sitting on your desk in no time."

I glanced back at Harry and was dumbfounded to see that he already had the two plastic bimbos practically lying in his lap. I saw my life flash before my eyes at that moment. I took a deep breath, afraid that I might pass out as I exited the restaurant. Some part of me knew that getting involved with Harry was the worst mistake of my life.

On my way back to the garage an excited fan walked up to me. "Hey! Aren't you the *Angry Movie Guy*?"

I looked at him and replied, "Hey! Aren't you the guy from the erectile dysfunction commercial?"

The man looked at me confused. "No, no I'm not."

I looked at him inquisitively. "Really? You have the same lacking emasculated 'je ne sais quoi', my mistake." I shrugged my shoulders and walked past him leaving the poor fellow dumbstruck.

Moments later a bus passed by with an ad of my show plastered on its side. It said: *Angry Movie Guy* "I give this film two thumbs down and the middle finger!" Next to it was a picture of me with a sarcastic loathing expression on my face.

I rushed home and immediately passed out on the couch. That night I slept like a baby. In truth, I slept soundly three nights in a row.

When I woke I thought maybe walking down memory lane wasn't so stupid after all. I felt a sense of renewal. I was ready to take on the world, or at least the independent film market. I hated being an asshole, but the world loved it so much that I stopped arguing with the facts of life and took it on as a persona. Truth be told, when I was a regular Joe I couldn't get a job. I spent two years of my life searching for work as a movie critic, bumming off my father and every other person I came across just to stay afloat. I finally started writing peoples obituaries to earn a living. I was basically suicidal at that point in my life, so I thought why not? At least this way I could write my own obituary before I stuck a knife into my heart. All of my life's work seemed to be meaningless until I met Harry. The truth of the matter is I felt that I owed the guy. Harry was my one stroke of luck! No matter how much I hated my life presently, it was better than what it was in the past.

I recollected the nightmare I had about my college graduation. I'd invited my father to the ceremony because it was the right thing to do. Besides whom else was I going to invite? My aunt Hilda had passed away from a stroke the year before I graduated. And boy was she lucky that I was on the phone with her when it happened, otherwise she would have become cat food. Her tattered estate was left to me in her last will and testament, as well as fifty cats that needed to be fed and taken care of. I turned the estate into an animal rescue, selling off all the valuables and using the life insurance policy to set up a fund to feed and take care of her cats and other strays that were brought in.

As much as I hated living with my great aunt Hilda I couldn't help growing fond of some of her odd ways. The first was her intense love of saving stray cats and the second was her passion for old Hollywood movies. She watched those movies like it was her religion, but no matter how good the actress was in the movie she would always say that my mother would have played the role better. After the end of every movie she would drag out all her old scrapbooks and show me all her glamorous publicity stills.

My Mother was a vision of perfection with her carefully painted on red lips and long auburn wavy hair. The reviews my mother received over the years were just as perfect as she was. Every one of those appraisals seemed like they were paying tribute to my mother and her talent. This was the drive behind my aspiration to be a movie critic.

As college graduation approached I listened to the other kids on campus talk of parties that they would attend and their plans for after graduation. I felt hopeless. I hadn't been invited to any party and my only guest at my graduation was my father who thought my dream of being a movie critic was the most ridiculous thing he had heard in his entire life.

After graduation, I strained to appear happy as I squeezed all two hundred and twenty pounds of bodyweight into the back seat of my father's favorite convertible. My father's girlfriend, Yasmine sighed as she tried to adjust her chair so that she could resume staring at herself in the flip-up vanity mirror. She obviously wasn't happy that I was there and she didn't seem concerned with keeping up appearances when it came to my own well-being. My father on the other hand was practically having a hernia trying to make her smile. He yelled back to me while he drove.

"You're going to love this place kid. Amazing sushi."

I felt pained by my father's remark. "I'm allergic to fish."

My father appeared annoyed by my comment, rather than sorry for making such an insensitive mistake. He yelled, "What? That's crazy!"

Yasmine also seemed annoyed. She rolled her eyes at me and continued to fix her make up using a small compact mirror she had pulled out of her Louis Vuitton handbag. After glossing her lips with three tubes of lip balm she shut her mirror and snuggled up to my father.

"I can't wait! I've been dying to try this restaurant. It's featured in Harper's Bazaar magazine!"

Then she turned around and batted her long fake eyelashes at me. I feigned a smile to Yasmine's relief and she turned back around and grabbed Ray's arm.

"Your father went to great lengths to get us a reservation so you could have your graduation dinner here. The least you could do is appreciate his efforts."

I swallowed hard as I listened to Yasmine while I simultaneously stared at her pillowy bosoms in the wing mirror.

My father turned the car hard and the tires squealed. He pulled into a parking lot where a young college student parked his convertible Porsche. The young valet couldn't help but notice Yasmine's nubile body feeding my father's already enormous ego. My father wrapped his arm around Yasmine's tiny waist and grabbed her buttocks to get under both the valet's and my skin.

The Japanese restaurant my father chose had a gaudy 80's décor. It clashed with the classic Japanese design. People from all walks of life were seated at one enormous table and a flurry of hands passed a massive assortment of sushi back and forth. My father and Yasmine were seated at the far end of the table and seemed oblivious of everyone else. I felt small, uncomfortable and out of place despite this supposedly being my big night. A group of waiters appeared at my side and opened several bottles of Veuve Clicquot and served my father's thirsty guests.

My father stood and raised his glass to make a boastful toast. "To my son Charlie! I can't say that I see much of a future critiquing movies but people tell me you're good at it. Still it doesn't seem like a job any self-respecting man would want, but hey different strokes for different folks. Am I right?" He looked around the table to be sure everyone was listening and then he continued. "And just know that when you fall on your ass you can always get your real estate license like your dear old dad and make something of yourself."

Yasmine yelled out, "To Charlie!"

All the other guests followed, "To Charlie!"

I looked around at everyone seated at the table with a bewildered look of confusion. I turned to my father. "Dad, who are all these people?"

He scoffed at me and continued to clink his glass with the rest of the crowd that was completely drunk and ignoring me with their chattering. I'd spent the last three hours of my party completely bored and looking like a child left alone amongst adults. Hours had passed and still I hadn't mustered up the nerve to excuse myself.

My father finished off his champagne and held up his glass to the waiter. He noticed me eyeing the door and called me over. "So Chucky boy, what are the big plans for the future?"

I looked confused, "Huh?"

He sarcastically slowed down his speech and spoke as though speaking to an impaired person. "Your plans for the future?"

I was baffled by my father's display and began to stutter. "Oh well, I… I uh…"

Before I could spit out a complete sentence Yasmine walked back from the bathroom wiping her nose. She was coked up and raring to go. The waiter followed her with more champagne. My father put his arms around Yasmine's waist and yelled at the top of his lungs so that the entire table could hear him.

"So one day a fat kid wants to be in the movies. He goes to an agent. Why does the agent decide to accept him?"

A guest from the table piped up. "I don't know? Why does the guy accept him?"

I watched in disbelief as my father smirked at me and then replied to the guest. "Because… he could fill a whole goddamn crowd scene by himself!"

My father started to laugh at his own joke and the rest of the table followed suit despite its lack of taste.

I began to laugh out of nervousness and accidentally developed my trademark saying right then and there.

"Crackers! That's just crackers!"

My father glared at me and then continued to address the rest of the table. "So who is up for dessert?"

Yasmine giggled at his complete disregard for me and raised her finger to acknowledge she was in. He grabbed her and began kissing her like a teenager in heat.

I was disgusted by their childish display and decided to take the opportunity to bolt for the door. I was almost out the gate when my father caught me. He pulled out his wallet and handed me ten one hundred dollar bills.

"Here is your graduation gift son."

I stared down at the money and then back up at my father. "Hey, at least you remembered my size this time."

I was surprised he let the barb slide and forced the money into my hands. He looked into my eyes. "Your mother would have been proud of you. She was into that stuff, movies and all of that."

I stared at him like he was completely un-recognizable. "Yeah, I know Dad."

My father turned around to leave and then stopped himself. "You should celebrate Son. You'll be playing with the big dogs soon enough. Pray you don't get bitten." Then my father slapped me on the back and began to bark like a dog. "Woof! Woof! Woof!"

I watched as my father walked away to rejoin his crowd of friends, never seeing the hurt expression on my face. The group cheered his name as he approached the table and it echoed through out the restaurant, making me want to vomit.

I bolted out of the restaurant, stuffing the cash into my pocket, hoping to never experience another moment like that again in my life.

WHO AM I?

Chapter Four

It was a Saturday and I had no plans… except to appear at the independent movie, "Four Golden Stars." Did they really want me to pick on the little guy? I mean, isn't it bad enough they liked watching me tear apart big Hollywood Stars, but now they wanted me to tear apart first timers. I felt weak. I thought maybe just once Harry would show me some compassion. I decided to ring him.

"Hello?"

"Hello Harry. It's Charlie."

Harry screamed into the phone. "What's cooking, good looking? You ready for tonight's shindig!?"

"What's that?" I said. "It's very loud wherever you are. I can't hear you."

Harry screamed again. "I said, what is cooking, good looking!"

"Oh, nothing much. Listen Harry, I'm not going to be able to make it to tonight's thing."

"What's that partner? Did you just say you're not going to make it tonight?" "That's what I said Harry. I'm not feeling well."

"Hold on a minute Charlie. I've got to get out of this crowd. I can't make out a word you're saying."

I waited for Harry as he strutted through the crowd of half naked women attending the pool party he was at. Finally, the noise subsided and Harry informed me that he had entered a hallway closet. I imagined him amidst an array of expensive women's shoes in his Bermuda shorts holding his rustled cowboy hat in one hand and a fruity cocktail in the other. Harry responded.

"It sounded like you said you're not going to make it out tonight Charlie."

"That is what I said."

"Holy Toledo Charlie, have you lost your mind? First, you keep me waiting at the bar for over an hour and now you've got me tied up in a hallway closet giving me a load of BS about not attending tonight's event."

I paused. "The thing is Harry… I really don't feel well."

"You're killing me Charlie. Listen, I didn't want to tell you this, but you've forced me. The Hollywood executives set this up. Hell! They dropped the damn ticket off at my apartment with a note that said: 'I can't wait to see how he'll react to this one.' They specifically said, "Let's see him pan the little guy." They want to see how America is going to react. So give them what they want and if it goes well the movie deal is signed and we're both set for life."

I feigned a cough. "And if it fails?"

"Charlie boy, failure is not in my vocabulary and since I am the one producing the show it is not in your vocabulary either. Now go get yourself a bit of fresh air. Or better yet, why don't you come visit me at this party? There are some really hot babes here. There is this one girl in the spa and you wouldn't believe the size of her bazookas."

Click. I hung up the phone. I looked at myself in the mirror and then changed into a pair of shorts and a t-shirt.

The phone rang. It was Harry calling me back. "Hello?"

"Did you hang up on me, Charlie?" Harry seemed agitated so I lied.

"No, why would I do that? We must have gotten disconnected…. I'm going to take your advice Harry."

"That a boy! So you want the address to the party?"

"No, but I will get out and get some fresh air. I think that should do the trick."

"Okay, if you say so buddy, but you're missing out on some real fine babes. So we're straight about tonight then, right? You are going to be there with bells on?"

"That's right Harry."

"Okay, well thanks for understanding. Break a leg amigo!"

I hung up the phone and dashed outside. Luckily, I didn't live too far from the park. I wasn't in the mood to do too much walking. On the way to the park I decided to stop for an iced mocha and a crème filled doughnut. While Harry filled himself up on young hotties, I romanced the female Indian doughnut clerk at the local Dunkin Doughnuts.

"So are there any specials today? Like maybe a two for one that I don't know about?"

"No sir, just what it says on the sign above me."

Strangely I felt at peace as I glanced up at an array of delectable diabetic deserts.

"So there is no delicious special on an iced macchiato?"

The woman looked annoyed. "As I said sir, it's just what it says on the sign above me."

I sighed. "In that case I'll take number six, but instead of the iced coffee can you make it an iced macchiato with extra whipped cream and chocolate on top." I wished I could resist ordering the most delicious thing on the menu, but no matter how hard I tried I found myself doing all the **Do Not's** on my diet.

I sat down at a table surrounded by teenagers. I stared out the window to avoid making eye contact with the riff raff. As I stuffed my face, I began to recall how I had been forced to go on a diet after being rushed to the hospital from the set of the *Angry Movie Guy*.

It was years ago, but I still remember being strapped to that hospital bed like it was yesterday. I was doing one of my long taping sessions. I was supposed to film four reviews in one day and I had just gone into my dressing room for a short break. While on break, I answered a phone call from my father who had blocked his caller id. He immediately started in on me.

"So you think because you're a big star now you don't have to answer the phone to speak to your father?" I looked down at my phone and realized my avoidance had finally caught up to me.

"Ray!" I said.

"I thought I told you to never call here unless you have an emergency. Is this an emergency?" At that very moment I became faint and passed out in my dressing room. Ray heard a loud crashing sound and he started calling out my name.

"Charlie? Charlie, are you okay?"

Astral Charlie emerged from my body unaware of what was happening.

I take it my father called the studio because minutes later a young male crewmember opened my dressing room door to check on me. He found me passed out on the ground.

On the way to the hospital I thought I was dying. My life was flashing before my eyes.

"I knew I wouldn't live to see sixty." I said, as I began to fade in and out of consciousness.

Astral Charlie was terrified. He began to pick up every device he saw in the back of the ambulance and hand it to the attendant who ignored his gestures.

"This is the problem with being Astral, no one takes you serious!"

Astral Charlie flew to my side and whispered into my ear. "Charlie don't leave me now, we haven't taken that trip to Tahiti. You promised we would go. Do something for him! We're losing him! I mean me!" Astral Charlie picked up the defibrillator in a frantic attempt to jump-start my heart.

My eyes rolled back in my head as I had a flash back of my youth. I was two years fresh from college and miserable. I had applied for every job in town that was in my field and had been turned down. Going to one of the best schools in the Country helped me achieve the interview of my dreams, but it had little effect over my potential employers desire to hire me.

I was on my way to the New Yorker. I had an interview with Nancy Prescott, a fifty-something-ish sophisticated woman with a low raspy voice and a tendency to flick her nails when she became agitated.

Nancy sat across from me at her enormous mahogany desk in her immaculate brown tailored pantsuit leafing through a folder of my work. She looked up at my eager face.

"You do realize that other than your reviews from your school paper you have nothing but obituaries in here?"

I was sweating bullets, but I forced myself to smile.

"Yes, I wrote and I researched each one myself. Their families were all very pleased."

Mrs. Prescott's nostrils began to flare and she began to flick her nails. "How gloomy. Do you have any real world experience Charlie? That is other than writing people's obituaries?" I knew this was my one shot at impressing Mrs. Prescott. I dabbed my forehead with a tissue and leaned forward.

"I know those reviews are not in some fancy paper or magazine like the New Yorker Mrs. Prescott, but those babies caused quite a stir at my school. I think if you just give me a chance you'll see what I mean..." Before I could finish Mrs. Prescott cut me off.

"Ever been published by a real newspaper, Mr. Zimmerman?" She stuck a Virginia Slim between her lips, lit it and blew a plume of smoke in my direction.

My eyes fluttered and began to tear from the smoke. "No, but those reviews had a big effect on what the students went to see." I tried not to cough as the smoke filled my face.

"Of course they did."

As the smoke cleared I saw Mrs. Prescott's wrinkled, menacing face and I knew that I had absolutely no shot at landing this job. Nancy stood up and started walking towards the door, but it didn't stop me from trying to promote myself. I picked up my coat trying to remain calm even though all I wanted to do was cry. I followed Nancy to the door.

"Did you know I even had a bit of a following?"

Nancy opened the door and guided me into the hallway watching me struggle to put on my tattered coat.

"I'll be frank kid, in the real world magazines depend on advertisers who are lured in by circulation numbers that are fueled by insightful and well-known contributors." She handed me back my folder.

"Sadly Mr. Zimmerman, you are not one of those contributors. Why don't you come back when you have some experience?"

Hoping to leave a good impression I stuck my hand out to shake Mrs. Prescott's, but my voice began to quiver and then crack.

"Thank you for seeing me Mrs. Prescott I really appreciate...." That was as far as I got before Mrs. Prescott slammed the door in my face.

The harsh sound of the door slamming in my face made me wake up. I grabbed one of the paramedics by the arm and screamed, "Did I have the big one?" The paramedic looked alarmed.

"The big what?"

"You know, the big one. Did I have a debilitating stroke or at least a heart attack?"

"No Mr. Evans! You are going to be just fine. We are headed to Mount Sinai Hospital and everything is going to be okay. It was just a panic attack."

"A panic attack! I just had a panic attack?" I felt humiliated. The mere thought of how I must have looked in front of the executives at the studio nearly caused me to have another attack.

Astral Charlie interrupted. "That's great news Charlie. Looks like we're going to Tahiti after all."

I passed out again as an image of me on the front page of the tabloids flashed before my very eyes. This time I drifted back to when I was living in lower Manhattan's Little Italy just off of Canal Street. I was a total mess. I stared out of the window of my dingy sixth-floor walk up apartment that smelled of cat piss. I spotted my friend Mahabahu, who I called Max for short. Max was a cheery Indian man of diminutive stature who had a strong odor that I later found out was the curry he ate profusely. Max sold newspapers on the corner of my block. I had pretty much given up on finding a job. I was miserable and hopeless, six months behind on rent and owed almost everybody money, including Max who I was about to hit up for another twenty bucks just so I could give one last stab at landing work as a critic. I put on my dogged Converse, which had seen better days and walked down the stairs over to Max's bustling newsstand. I could smell curry as I approached him.

"Hi Max."

Max spoke with an Indian drawl.

"Hey Charlie! Any luck with a job?" I shook my head. "No… not yet, but I can feel my destiny beginning to change." I picked up the New York Times, a Filmmaker magazine and a Variety magazine.

Max eyed me. He knew I couldn't afford to pay him. "Pay me on Friday Charlie?"

I nodded my head. "Thanks. I appreciate it."

Max shrugged it off. "Don't worry about it. You'll catch your break bro."

I smiled at Max as he tried to pick up on the American slang. I felt tired and worn out; there were bags under my eyes. I shrugged my shoulders. "My luck will change."

Max banged the counter with his fist. "Darnit Charlie, you make your own luck in this world. Do you think I got all this just by being lucky?" Max spread his arms wide to indicate his entire newsstand. "You can't be a doormat your entire life," he said with an arrogant grin on his face.

"I'm not a doormat Max!"

"Bull shittt kiddo, you might as well wear a jacket with a welcome sign stitched on to the back of it." Max put a loving arm around my shoulder. "You got to be more cutthroat if you're going to make it in America! It's a dog-eat-dog world."

I looked at Max as if he was from another planet. "Everybody else is like that. I'm going to be different Max."

Max shook his head. "Drop the Mr. Rogers act. People don't want nice. They want to see a train wreck. They want to see blood on the dance floor... I mean street."

I stared at Max like he had just sunk my last battleship. I picked up my bag of newspapers.

"I'll see ya on Friday Max. And don't worry about me. Things are looking up."

Max busted out singing a rendition of Diana Ross's famous song "I will survive." He was off key and singing it with an Indian accent, but it was still impressive. It was also a significant turning point in my life. Max's singing jarred me out of my deep sleep; I awoke in a hospital bed in Mount Sinai with tubes and apparatuses coming out of every part of me. The next two days were miserable. I spent them lying in the hospital taking every test known to mankind all because I had answered an anonymous phone call from my father.

On the flip side, Astral Charlie was having a great time. He was doing his best to influence my waking life by taking the opportunity to explore the medical field. He couldn't fathom how many diseases I could catch or might already have. When the nurse would order a few tests to run on me Astral Charlie would check off a few more. I felt nauseous every time the nurse walked in and asked me to pee into a cup. Sure I was little overweight, forty something and on anti-depressants, but I felt moderately healthy despite the fact that I just had a panic attack when my emotionally un-available father called. I reviewed the tests with the doctor. The test results were conclusive of my un-healthy lifestyle.

My doctor stared at my chart. "You should take better care of yourself Charlie. You're on your way to writing your own death sentence."

Suddenly, I snapped back into reality and observed my surroundings. The Dunkin Donut's I was sitting in was jammed packed with creepy looking teenagers and old people who stared at me with disdain. I looked down and noticed that I had devoured two glazed doughnuts and an iced macchiato, but I still felt hungry. I decided to leave before ordering again. Dr. Bloom's two hundred dollar an hour analysis had determined that my overeating was a result of suppressing my emotions from the past.

I spotted an empty park bench across the street from Dunkin Donut's and walked over to sit down. Joggers and bikers were passing by; I wondered if I could ever be like them? A heavy jogger ran by sweating like a pig. I blanketed my eyes from the sight of him. What's the use? I thought to myself as I dozed off into a deep lethargic slumber and woke up in an absurd dream.

I was running through a forest, but it was not like I was on a brisk jog in the park, it was as if I was being chased! In the distance I could hear the sound of dogs approaching and I began to panic. I felt my heart racing.

"Dammit!" I screamed as I ran down a hill listening to the sound of the dogs barking grow louder. I looked behind me. Were they gaining on me? I wondered. To my relief I spotted a small cabin a few meters away.

I heard a man's voice. "We're coming to get you Charlie!"

I ran harder and faster, wondering where it was coming from. My instincts told me all I had to do was get to the cabin and it would be okay. Entering the small wooden cabin I bolted the door shut. Looking around me I saw a gun hanging over the fireplace and another by the door. I grabbed one of the weapons as I peered out the window.

A deadly battlefield had morphed outside the cabin and I was now a soldier in a war. A kid who appeared to be no older than twenty stood beside me in full military gear. The young blue-eyed soldier grabbed my pistol and shouted. "I don't care what it takes. I'm not going out like this!"

I felt like I was suffocating under the weight of my helmet so I removed it. I was stunned to find that the cabin was packed wall to wall with soldiers.

"Where the hell am I?" I wondered aloud.

A group of militant soldiers glared at me. One of the soldiers with a deep scar under his left eye spoke to me. "Have you lost your damn mind Son? You are a soldier in the United States Army and we are in the middle of battle. Take a look!"

The lieutenant grabbed me by the shoulder blade and forced me to look out the window. "We are surrounded soldier! If you don't want to die I suggest you put your God damn helmet back on and pick up that rifle! Assume the position soldier!"

My dream seemed to be put on pause as my mind tried to assess what was going on.

"Holy shit!" I mumbled to myself.

I had miraculously been transported into a movie I had reviewed. Standing in front of me was Oscar winner MATT BARKER! I thought to myself, I never expected to be in the movies with a gut and all. This dream was turning out better than I imagined. Stumbling around the cabin I began looking for a script. I murmured. "Shit, what's the next line?"

I was beginning to panic. "Forget it," I muttered to myself. "I'll just make it up as I go, isn't that what James Dean did?"

I screamed at Matt. "We're not getting out of this alive soldier! You and I both know that!" I tried to incorporate the lessons my mother had taught me as a boy, but I wasn't sure the soldiers were buying my half-witted attempt at method acting. I gazed into Matt's piercing blue eyes.

"I've seen this a thousand times. This is our last chance!" I was really getting into the role now. "If you boys have any last words you best say them now!"

Matt eye balled the muddy troop of men bizarrely and then turned back to me with a hard stare. I had appeared out of nowhere in this scene and I could tell that Matt was taken back. He didn't know how to handle the situation, but I knew what I needed to do. Putting my hand on Matt's shoulder I confessed my sins. "Look Matt… I'm sorry for being a total douche bag. I didn't mean what I said. You're not a second rate actor in a first rate film. I know that now because I can see you up close in front of all these cameras and bright lights. Can you ever forgive me? Matt?"

Matt took two steps back and turned towards the other actors playing soldiers. "Who the hell is this idiot?"

There was dead silence on set, you could hear a pin drop. I heard the cameras rolling and I felt like Clint Eastwood in a big blockbuster film. I picked up my weapon like a veteran soldier and looked around at the other actors.

"Forget it boys. I can handle this one." I tried to stay in character, keeping a straight face as I rambled on. "No one has to do my dirty work. I ripped Matt's performance to shreds and I didn't speak very highly of any of you either. Actually, I think I said, I'd seen better acting in a re-make of Grease at my high school play."

The actors started to get pissed off and walk off the set, but Matt stopped them abruptly. "Hold on a minute... I want to see where he's going with this one."

I smiled with great relief. "Thanks for understanding Matt."

"Don't thank me yet," he said. There was dead silence in the room.

I feigned a nervous laugh. "Right, you see... the thing is Matt, I didn't mean it. They pay me you realize to act like an asshole."

Matt Barker's helmet slipped out of his hand. "Now I remember you!"

I swallowed hard watching the veins pop out of Matt's neck.

"Man! That was you? You're a real moron! I ought to shove this helmet so far down your throat!" Matt picked up his helmet and shook it in my face.

"I know... I know Matt." I said, cowering in front of him as he struggled to free himself from two husky soldiers who were holding him back. "Listen, I was wrong man. This is Academy Award winning acting!"

Matt stopped dead in his tracks, softened by my comment. "You really think it's good enough to be a contender at the Oscars?"

I nodded my head. "Yes, I do, and I'm not just saying that because you can pummel me to the ground."

Matt clenched his jaw and flexed his bicep at me. "That's right... you better believe it." Matt smirked at the crew and then looked back at me. "How the hell did you get in here anyway?"

"I don't know?" I said, as I sheepishly looked around the room at the other men. "I think I'm dreaming or maybe it's another hallucination." The muddy troop of men stared at me indignantly. "You see ever since I met the woman of my dreams and then discovered she was nothing but a figment of my imagination I've sort have been having a meltdown."

All the men collectively sighed and then the young blue-eyed soldier mumbled, "Man, that's horrible."

I shook my head in agreement and picked up my rifle. "Never in my life did I think I would be such an angry movie guy."

Matt looked confused. "What?"

"Never mind," I said, putting on my helmet and moving towards the cabin door. "I want you all to know that I have come to terms with the fact that I'll never see the woman of my dreams again, which makes what I'm about to do easier."

The men clapped joyously following Matt's lead.

"I know I'm destined to live out my days alone, which frankly makes life not worth living!" I dramatically opened the door of the cabin and ran into the middle of the battlefield where several men in opposition gunned me down. I began to jerk in my sleep from the bullets hitting me in my dream.

I was about to fall off the park bench I was sitting on when a small child standing next to me pointed at me and screamed. "Mommy, mommy... what's wrong with that guy?"

I opened my eyes and wiped the drool hanging from my mouth. I saw the young boy and realized where I was.

"Oh shit, shit, shit...!"

The mother of the young boy covered her son's ears and scurried away scolding me. "You ought to be ashamed of yourself cursing in front of a young boy."

I grabbed my iPhone from my pocket to check the time. My nap put me an hour behind schedule. I ran back to my apartment and changed into a new pair of Levi jeans and a dark pin stripped button down shirt. Minutes later, I bolted out the front door with my favorite Roberto Cavalli jacket. I left with just enough time to make it to the indie film premiere at the NY Indie Film Festival. The tires on my Porsche squealed as I maneuvered into the parking garage.

Everything was a blur as I ran towards the theatre; my heart was pounding as I ran right past HER! Standing there on the exterior footsteps of the theater was the fiery redheaded woman I'd met at the special engagement of *Lost in Her Eyes*. As I hit the threshold of the theatre doors I realized whom it was and I turned around and sprinted back down the stairs shouting.

"It's you!"

She turned around. "Are you talking to me?"

I exclaimed, "You're her! You're that woman from the movie engagement. You don't remember meeting me at, *Lost in Her Eyes*, starring Edie Greene and Jack Waters?"

"Oh! You're him! You're that guy. It's so nice to see you again." She smiled. "What a coincidence, it's at another movie theatre."

"The movieee!" I blurted it out like a crazy person while grabbing my head.

She looked alarmed. "Yes, you're at a movie theatre. Are you alright?"

"I'm okay? It's just that I have to go, err… to the movies…err, I mean someone is expecting me."

Her soft brown eyes, complimented her contagious smile. "Oh, I see?"

I was beaming from ear to ear as spoke to her. "I would love to stay and chat with you, but if I don't leave right now I'm going to be in a lot of trouble."

She stopped smiling. "Oh… your girlfriend?"

"No, no, no! That's not it. Actually, I'm single at the moment. Free like a bird!" I mimicked a soaring bird, which looked more like a demented chicken. She laughed as I stumbled around the steps of the theatre, crashing into her and knocking her over. Luckily, my quick reflexes saved the day. I caught her in the knick of time. As I stared into her soft brown eyes I began to blush. I knew I had to ask her out.

"I would really like to take you out. Can we talk sometime… maybe?" I handed her my business card and she smiled at me as I glanced down at my watch. "Shit! I really have to go! You'll call me, right?"

She nodded her head and I blew her a kiss as I raced up the stairs of the theatre shouting, "You really have no idea how happy I am to see you!" She waved goodbye smiling as I stumbled on the last step.

Entering the theatre, I bolted into the Cineplex that was showing, *Four Golden Stars*, by Alex Rasner. I looked around the crowded theater for my seat. Hidden in the back of the theatre I spotted my assistant Samantha. She was sitting with her date, an affable tall all American young man named Ryan whom she introduced to me at last year's holiday party. I observed Samantha sink down in her seat at the sight of me, elbowing Ryan to do the same. Ryan looked at her baffled and then ducked down in his chair. Her attempt to avoid me made me smirk because I knew I was not the type of boss an employee wants to see outside of work.

I continued to search for my seat in the dim theatre lighting. I scanned the best areas of the cinema for the reserved seating, but every seat was taken. As I walked down the aisle Astral Charlie emerged from my body like a ghost. He had learned how to escape by body during my waking conscious. He took one look at the crowded theatre and flew between the walls leaving me standing in the aisle.

Seconds later, the producer of the film Mr. Gary Clarkson, a debonair Armani clad Englishman walked toward me with his hand extended. "What a pleasure!"

I snarled at him. "Where's my seat?" I could tell Mr. Clarkson was startled by my rudeness.

"Of course, right your seat. Let's see?" He scanned the room for an empty seat eventually spotting one in the front of the theatre. "Yes! Of course it's right this way," he bellowed over a sea of chattering movie go'ers. Mr. Clarkson guided me down the aisle trying to strike up a conversation, but his nerves got the best of him. Eventually he paused in the middle of the aisle and turned to me and said in his crisp English accent, "I don't think I introduced myself. I'm the producer of the film, *Four Golden Stars*." Gary's left eye began to twitch as he watched the expression on my face become angrier.

I rolled my eyes and said, "That's just super Gary," as I desperately tried to keep my Angry Movie Guy persona in tact even though I felt like leaping and dancing with joy after seeing my dream girl.

I motioned for Gary to move it along. "Let's keep it moving, shall we?"

Gary looked down at his Rolex. "It's just that your reviews are…"

I cut Gary off. "Just so we're clear, pissing me off before I take my seat isn't going to help you with the review of this film."

Gary nodded his head. "Right, okay let me see. Its right this way." Gary rushed down the aisle as the lights lowered. A preview flickered on the movie screen. I could tell that Gary was trying to remain calm, but the situation was awkward. It was clear that his public relations staff failed to inform him that I would be attending tonight's premiere and Gary was doing his best to avoid embarrassment.

Gary spotted an empty seat and left me standing in the middle of the aisle looking like an idiot. "Excuse me Ma'am, could you please move your sweater and purse from that empty seat?"

I slid up to Gary. "You're joking, right?"

Gary shook his head, "No, why?"

I lost it. "Crackers! That's just crackers! You expect me to sit through an entire low budget indie film sandwiched between Deimos and Phobos?" Gary saw that my seat was in the middle of two morbidly obese African American women. The two baby-faced women were dressed in bright neon spandex and hissed and sucked as they attempted to remove the popcorn from in between their teeth. The woman kept looking back and forth at one other, annoyed because they had to move their fake Louis Vuitton bags from the empty seat.

Gary's voice trembled, "Deimos and who?"

Narrowing my brow, I blurted out "Moons! They are moons of Mars... you know what, forget it. The film is beginning."

Mr. Clarkson whispered, "I'm really sorry Mr. Evans this is the best I can do right now. Believe me, you won't even notice it once the lights are off and the movie starts." Gary grinned like a Cheshire cat and dashed up the aisle, leaving me standing there dumbstruck. I panned the theatre for another seat, but the theatre was packed. I reluctantly made my way to the seat.

"Pardon me. Excuse me. " I said to the first obese woman stuffing her face with a handful of greasy popcorn. "I need to get in there."

The woman sucked her teeth, rolled her eyes and wiggled in her seat making just enough room for one of my butt cheeks. I let out a nervous laugh to break the tension. "Crackers!"

Both women's heads snapped back as they spoke to one other. "What he just say?"

I ignored them. The tan body builder sitting in the row behind me was becoming irritated because he couldn't see the previews.

He leaned forward. "Hey buddy the movie is about to start! Are you going to sit down or what?"

His thick Philly accent reminded me of Sylvester Stallone in Rocky Balboa and I wanted to laugh, but instead I whispered, "If *Shamoo* and *Free Willy* would be so kind as to un-beach themselves I'd be delighted to do just that."

I took a deep breath, trying to suck in my belly as I eased myself into the seat the woman's legs were spilling into. "Excuse me Ma'am, could you move your ham for legs so I can sit?"

She didn't budge, instead one of them barked. "Ow! Be careful! There isn't room!"

Without skipping a beat I body slammed her with my words. "There would be room if you had a salad once in a while."

The woman glared at me. "Listen asshole, we came here to enjoy the movie. Not to be judged by you or anyone else."

I began to nervously laugh and said, "You fatties stick together, don't you?"

The woman's eyes bulged out of her head. "You're one to talk chubby."

Looking down I scoffed, "Chubby? I have a personal trainer who comes to my home three times a week!"

The women squealed and rolled their eyes. "To do what, cook?"

Glaring at her I said, "If only I had a snickers bar to shut you up." She gasped, as I tried to stand up, but my jacket was caught in the chair. "Dammit. I'm stuck!" I turned to the obese woman to the left of me. "Pardon me, but do you think you could reach your chubby little fingers behind me and unhook my jacket, please?"

She glared at me. "Kiss my ass fatso!"

I looked at her rear end. "All of it? Because I really don't have that kind of time." I turned towards the fat woman on my right. "What about you? There's a membership in it for Jenny Craig if you do it."

The woman looked me dead straight in the eye. "Drop dead!"

I went back to struggling with my coat. The movie had already begun and it was clear I was stuck. I let out another cry for help, "I'm stuck! Get me out of here!"

The woman to my left barked. "Just leave your coat and go already."

I looked at her with disdain. "It's a Roberto Cavalli. You do not leave behind a Roberto Cavalli jacket!"

The irate Sylvester Stallone look-a-like stood up and grabbed me by the shoulders. "Listen jackass, if you don't shut the hell up I am going to beat you senseless!" I inched down in my seat. The fat women began to clap and I demurely crossed my legs and hunkered down even lower into my chair. The muscle man scowled at me. "And keep your head down! Way down!"

He pushed my head so far down that I couldn't possibly see the screen. The fatties on either side of me piled their supersize soda cups, greasy bags of popcorn and milk duds next to my seat. As I sat there, pinned between two giant whales I imagined Gary frantically running out of the theatre to warn the director of the film. I could see him slapping whatever jackass made the VIP list.

I began to mutter to myself. "Who ever they are they better start looking for a new job because when I get finished with the review of this film they are through!"

Afraid for my life I didn't budge till the movie ended. As the lights came up I tugged on my jacket, ripping my favorite Robert Cavalli coat trying to escape. "Dammit!"

The baby faced woman on the right side of me stood up blocking my way and knocking a full size cherry soda down the front of my pants and onto my suede shoes.

"Oops, sorry," she said with an attitude.

"Damn it!" I sneezed. "That's it!" I screamed as I pushed past the woman. I mumbled, "Fucking Cretins!"

One of the women tried to grab me, but her friend held her back. "Don't even bother, he's not worth it!"

I saw Gary rushing into the theatre with a panicked expression on his face. "What's wrong, Mr. Evans? You look upset. I pushed past him in a rage grumbling to myself as I listened to Mr. Clarkson call after me. "Mr. Evans, if you leave now you'll miss the director!"

I stormed into the lobby wild eyed and on fire shrieking, "After that experience they should consider themselves lucky!" I rushed into the theatre entrance still struggling with my coat and I ran right into my dream girl.

"Hi!" I looked up. The woman of my dreams had me cornered. "Are you okay?" She said.

I was beguiled by her instantly and began to take on the characteristics of a bashful schoolboy.

She stuck out her hand examining the rip in my jacket. "What happened to you in there? You look like you were attacked by wild dogs!"

I was a complete disaster. "Uh, yeah…something like that. I'm fine, actually. Thank you." I tugged on the rip in my coat trying to cover the cherry coke stain down the front of my pants.

"Are you sure?"

I pulled on my coat. "Yeah, I'm great! This is how they're wearing their clothes in Milan this summer. It's the shredded look." I mocked a runway strut. She giggled as I continued to clown around like a love-struck fool. "I have to go. I hope… I mean I would appreciate seeing you again. Good-bye. Good luck!" She looked confused as I awkwardly dashed off.

Seconds later Astral Charlie flew out from the dark theatre yelling. "Wait! Where are you going Charlie? I haven't finished watching the new Darren Aronofsky film!"

Just then Mr. Clarkson sprinted up behind Alex almost spilling into her. "What just happened Lexi? Where did Mr. Evans go?"

Alex wrinkled her cute button nose. "I have no idea? He ran off before I had a chance to speak to him about the movie."

Mr. Clarkson slapped his forehead. "You didn't stop him?" Gary walked back inside the theatre moaning as Lexi tagged close behind him leaving Astral Charlie alone in the Cineplex.

WHAT THE HELL DO I WANT?

Chapter Five

I went straight home and watched *Lost in Her Eyes,* until I fell asleep and woke up in my dream as Jack Waters, the handsome and debonair actor in the film. It was New Years' Eve, and Jack Water's smoky art-deco nightclub was packed with tinsel towns finest! I felt like a king sitting at the head of the table in a well-tailored black pinstripe suit puffing on an expensive cigar surrounded by my handsome friends. All of my guests were dressed to the nines; each one wore a purple flower in their lapel to signify they were honored guests at my table.

I motioned for a pretty blonde cocktail waitress with a sweet tukus to take my order.

"Hello Mr. Waters. How can I help you?"

I smiled at her and tipped my black fedora. "Hello doll face. Do me a favor will ya…crack a few more bottles of the finest champagne in the house for my friends here and be quick about it. The ball is about to drop!"

The cute blonde cocktail waitress grabbed the empty ice bucket off of the table and scurried away. Minutes later, she returned with another pretty waitress who topped off everyone's glass. The men at my VIP table stood proudly by my side with their champagne flutes lifted as one of the men made a toast.

"To Jack! For throwing the best New Year's Eve celebration and of course for treating all of us fools!"

All the men clinked glasses and then sipped on the bubbly that was now over flowing.

From the glittering stage Bill, a longtime friend and the best jazz pianist I've ever heard held up his flute in triumph. I met Bill's intense gaze with my own and lifted my champagne flute to meet his. I motioned for the guys to raise their glasses as I toasted my good friend.

"To Bill Coleman of Bill Coleman and the Fancy Four."

Bill grabbed the microphone and addressed the crowd. "Is this thing on?" The crowd cheered, but Bill motioned for them to settle down. "We are about to start the countdown ladies and gentleman." I watched the dapper men at my private table disburse and begin bustling around the room looking for a beautiful woman to kiss at the stroke of midnight. Bill spoke into the microphone, but it was no longer transmitting sound. I could tell he was panicking, so I ran up to the stage and offered to help.

"Let me give it a try buddy."

I wiggled the cord and then whistled into the microphone. I watched as all eyes turned towards me. Mr. Coleman shrugged his shoulders and tipped his hat to me as he limped off the stage. I grabbed the microphone from the stand and held it close to my mouth. "Ladies and Gentleman, the ball is about to drop. Can I get you to raise your glasses and count down the New Year with me?" I scanned the room searching for Edie. Where in the world could she be, I thought to myself, while holding up my glass for the toast. I announced to the crowd. "Okay, here we go! Ten, nine, eight, seven, six, five, four, three, two one! Happy New Year!"

The room filled with confetti! The crowd hollered, clinking their champagne flutes and kissing their loved ones. I shouted into the microphone. "Happy New Year everyone. May 1946, be filled with love, laughter, and romance! And now, for the event you have all been waiting for. Coming to the stage, is the bright star we've all come to love and adore, the one, the only, Miss Edie Greene! Drum roll please!" The audience tapped on their candle lit tables, like they were playing a drum, until they saw Edie appear from behind the glittering curtain.

Edie swayed onto the stage wearing an off the shoulder black sequence gown with a deep v-cut in the back which accentuated her curvaceous bottom. Her porcelain skin glowed like a china doll against her red luscious locks. The crowd, especially the men went crazy at the mere sight of her. Edie blushed at their approval. I addressed the rowdy audience. "Miss Edie Greene is going to give you her best rendition of 'Aren't you Glad You're You,' by Miss Doris Day!"

Edie reached for the microphone, but before she could speak I yelled out, "My God, isn't she perfect in every way?" The crowd cheered in agreement as Edie soaked in their admiration.

Then Edie replied in her low-pitched sultry voice, "I've always admired a man who says what's on his mind."

I squeezed my eyes shut. "I never want to wake up!" Edie Greene had magically transformed into my dream girl from outside the movie premiere and somehow she was even more stunning than the actual Edie Greene. "Things are finally changing," I murmured to myself as I snuggled under the covers watching Edie sing to a room full of adoring fans. I whispered, "If I could steal just one dance with her I'd die a happy man!" She sang for what seemed like an eternity, but it was only minutes.

I beckoned to Bill to play something from Billy Holiday as I danced over to Edie's side. "Take my hand Edie."

Edie reached out her long satin black glove, but I brushed passed it and grabbed her tiny waist, twirling her onto the dance floor and into my arms. Bill began to play a few bars of Billie Holiday's, "I'll be seeing you," on the piano, while the crowd cheered. Soon the song faded into, "I only have eyes for you," by Harry Warren and finally Bill and the Fancy Four took over the stage. It was obvious to those watching in the crowd that I only had eyes for this woman. I danced with her till the lights went out in the club and the sun came up in my apartment. My alarm clock blared, jolting me out of a passionate waltz with my dream girl.

I leaped out of bed and ran to check how many business cards I had left in my wallet. "I have ten cards!" I shouted. "I had eleven business cards yesterday!" Dancing on the bed I professed, "She's alive! She's not some hysterical hallucination trying to overtake my world and land me in the loony bin." I fell to the floor and began banging on it, like a lunatic. "Yes! Thank you! Thank you! Thank you! You don't know how many times since I met this woman that

I've imagined myself being locked up in a loony bin and drugged up for all of eternity while being forced to rehash all the shitty reviews I've given over the years! But I don't have to anymore, because she's real!"

I rambled on and on to myself as I ran down the stairs of my two-story condo and into my modern stainless steel kitchen and began brewing a fresh pot of Columbian coffee. "Even better than being alive she actually seems to like me, that is of course if I didn't scare her off last night by acting like a complete moron!" I snarled as I over filled my bowl of Captain Crunch, only to realize that I had no milk. "Fuck, that stupid maid forgot to buy milk again! Why do I even pay her?" I pinched off a small amount of fish food into the fish bowl next to me where my Chinese fighting swordfish named Lucifer awaited with puckered lips. "Here you go Lucifer!" Picking up a small can of Purina cat food I stroked my favorite cat Rex as I began muttering to myself. "I can't believe this filmmaker! How stupid can you be? You don't reserve a seat for the biggest critic in town?" I scratched my ass. "Something doesn't add up? Had the network set me up? Or maybe... it was the Chinese movie executives wanting to make me look like an idiot!"

I sat down at the kitchen table in my boxer shorts and took a sip of my hot coffee. I contemplated, "On second thought, it wouldn't surprise me if Harry had plotted the whole scenario just so I would go into a rage on national television." I stormed back up stairs screaming to myself, "Fine, if a show is what they want, that is exactly what they will get! I will rip that movie to shreds just like they ripped my favorite Cavalli jacket!"

Searching through my walk-in closet I pulled out my favorite Hugo Boss suit and set it on the bed. "I got to be dressed to kill." I smiled like the Joker from Batman and quickly jumped in and out of a cold shower. I gave myself a half-ass shave before I changed from my birthday suit into my navy blue, double breasted, smok'em if you got'em, sex-machine of a getup. I felt like Jack Waters as I jived aloud, "Tomorrow's your birthday Charlie and this year you got something to live for!" I beamed from ear to ear as I jumped into my Porsche revving myself up for the show. "You've tasted love Charlie and it is better than any glazed crème filled doughnut." I looked into my rearview mirror and squinted my eyes, "Knock'em dead you handsome devil!"

I turned on the radio and Donna Summers hit song, *I Will Survive* began to play. Once again, my Indian friend Max popped into my head. I hummed along as I sat at the stoplight. As the song came to a close I screamed at the top of my lungs. "I'm in love!" I turned my head and peered into the SUV next to me to see if anyone had noticed my outburst. Sitting in the back seat was an obnoxious little girl with brunette pigtails talking on her cell phone like she was all grown up. Like most grown ups in my life she too appeared to despise me. She was giving me the evil eye, so I flipped her the bird! To my surprise, the little brat flipped me the bird back and mouthed the words "F.U. Stinky," while showing off her missing two front teeth. I pressed on the gas and sped off arriving ten minutes early to the studio thanks to successfully running three red lights.

As I strolled into the studio I observed my assistant Samantha muttering to herself as she paced the floors. "I bet that madman is going to try and end my cousin's career today." Samantha looked up as the door slammed shut. Her face was wrinkled with torment as she watched me stroll into the studio with a smile from ear to ear. Her agitation normally would have set me off, but I had already decided today was going to be different. I wasn't going to let my assistant, or anyone else for that matter, put me in a bad mood. I casually strolled towards my dressing room saying hello to everyone I came into contact with. "Good afternoon," I said to a big-breasted security guard I passed, not waiting for her to reply. I walked a few feet, passing by yet another employee I'd never bothered to greet. I arrogantly turned and said, "Hello Stan. How is my favorite security guard today?"

My pale co-worker replied, "It's John actually and I'm not in security, but good afternoon Charlie."

I smiled and replied, "That's right, John. It's good to see you. You look different. Did you get a haircut?"

John shook his head no as he watched me saunter off. Seconds later, I observed him shoot a peculiar look in Samantha's direction.

Samantha was shaking her head and waiving her hands while she mouthed the words, "Do not get me involved."

I approached Samantha and she stopped dead in her tracks. "Good afternoon Sa..ma..."

Samantha cut me off. "It's Samantha. You had it right, sir."

I smiled and said, "Well it's good to see you Samantha. I am so happy that you could be here this afternoon and thank you for getting me my coffee every day and running my errands for me."

Samantha's jaw dropped and John walked over to her side and picked it up. I grinned as my astonished co-workers tried to remain calm. I said, "Well I better get going, there's a show to be made!" Then I slid away humming the tune to, *I Will Survive*.

As the door of my dressing room shut I noticed John ushering Samantha into a quiet corner, but my normal paranoid thoughts did not enter my brain. I looked into the mirror and spoke to myself. "Did you see the look on their faces? That was priceless!" I was beaming with joy as I sat down in my plush leather chair waiting for the on-set hair and make-up artist to arrive. Moments later, Cecilia opened the door of my dressing room and began to powder my nose and fix my hair. As I sat there being made up my mind began to wander. I started to imagine what those two nitwits were saying about me. Luckily, my astral self had stayed behind to spy for me.

Astral Charlie flew over to Samantha's side to listen in on their conversation.

John whispered, "Can you believe he said hello to me Sam and he actually seemed sincere about it?"

Sam squinted her eyes. "Yeah, I know. Do you think he was abducted by aliens last night?"

John smirked, "It's either that or someone slipped something into his iced macchiato?"

Sam shook her head. "Don't look at me. I'm completely innocent...this time."

They burst out laughing, but then Samantha abruptly stopped. "I don't trust him. He's up to no good. I've worked here for two years and Charlie's never as much as glanced at me! Unless of course it was to yell at me, humiliate me, or return his damn coffee!"

John put his hand on Sam's shoulders. "Well, maybe he's changed Sam? People change."

Sam put her hand on her hip. "Yeah people change, but Charlie isn't people. The network hired Charlie to spruce up the news broadcast station and when it worked they went into shock and handed him over his own show. Charlie is a troll that somebody let onto national television because they needed ratings."

John looked shocked. "Man... you really seem to have thought that one through."

Sam shook her head. "No, I just know people like him."

"I thought you said Charlie wasn't people Samantha?"

Samantha rolled her eyes as she blew a strand of her blonde hair out of her face. "He isn't John. You'll see. I've prepared myself for the worst. Charlie's not going to sucker punch me. I know he is going to rip Alex's film to shreds." Samantha picked up her clipboard and walked over to the monitor.

By this point I had managed to lower the volume on the normal paranoid thoughts going through my brain. I rushed out of my dressing room and whizzed by Astral Charlie as I pulled off my make-up bib. I strutted onto set. I felt radiant until out of the

85

corner of my eye I saw Samantha mouth the words to John, "Don't be fooled, he's psycho!" Her words hit me like a ton of bricks, confirming my paranoid suspicions were not simply paranoia. I snapped back into *Angry Movie Guy* reality ready to give the film the worst review in the history of mankind.

I glanced back at Samantha and she looked terrified. I couldn't figure out why she was so upset about me doing my job. This must be her time of the month or maybe it's drugs? That's it! I concluded. I bet my assistant is on some new upper-downer drug that leaves you smiling one moment and on your knees crying the next.

The stage manager yelled out, 'Five, four, three, two, one and we're on the air."

I flashed my normal cheesy sardonic smile at the camera showing off my porcelain white veneers before bursting into my review. "Another week and yet another two hours of my life that I'll never be able to get back folks! All you film buffs know that its film festival season, so I thought I'd get out there and see what some of the indie filmmakers are up to. Truth be told, I wouldn't know what they had to offer because I was held hostage between two feeding whales! Such a shame!" I twirled towards the camera and pointed my finger at the home audience. "I'm sure all of you at home are wondering what I'm talking about? Well let me elaborate. I was supposed to see *Four Golden Stars*, by writer and director Alex Rasner, whom ever he is? But I never saw anything, although I heard plenty!" I stuck my finger down my throat. "What nonsense!"

I swiveled my chair towards camera two and saw Samantha's face contort as she listened to my vehement critique. I watched her scribble something into her logbook while she mimed the words *I Quit* to John. She then motioned for John to take over at the monitor and she ran off the set. Screw her! I thought, as I continued my brilliant vitriolic criticism.

"This was by far the worst chick-flick since *Steel Doves*. And for all you sicko's who are thinking, 'I loved *Steel Doves* why don't you just do us all a favor and go vomit on your LEFT foot!' *Four Golden Stars* was TRASH, without zest! God help us all when we give the camera over to a blind retard. The only thing worse would have been to hand it over to a woman!" I took a sip from my mug of coffee and then sprayed it out at the camera. "For the love of God, I haven't been able to get the taste of cinematic failure out of my mouth since I left that movie! Frankly, I feel violated. The New York Indie Film Frenzy Festival...Crackers! This was more like a charity event for the Special Olympics." I paced to and fro making it hard for the cameraman to keep me in frame. "And the Gold Medal goes to Alex Nastier. Unbelievable! What I heard of the acting was trite and unfeeling. The storyline was no better than that of a pretentious first year film student at a community college!" I snapped my fingers at the crew. "I'm not finished. So just take a seat ladies and gents in T.V. land, because I've got another forty minutes of R rated ranting about this piece of garbage. Forget about the other films I'm supposed to review. This is personal." I ranted on and on soaking up every last minute of the show with my venomous tirade and then decided to end it with the following, "I'd watch your back Nasty Rasner. I'll be waiting for you in the tall grass with a billiard ball in a sock! This is Angry Movie Guy sounding off... I give this pathetic excuse of a film two thumbs down and the middle finger!" I flipped the bird at the camera and then walked off set, but my tirade wasn't over. I pointed at the director who was rolling his eyes at me and yelled. "Hey! I saw that. If it weren't for me you would still be directing game shows! So look alive!"

I watched my assistant Samantha reappear and tug on John's shirt before ducking behind the monitor. Her annoying little preppy voice started going off in my head again. "Oh my God! See what I mean? He's lost it. His niceness was just a prelude to his pre-adolescent desire to degrade another human being."

John looked over his steel wire framed glasses at the monitor and mouthed the words. "It will be okay, Sam."

I threw my microphone on the floor and flew by Samantha and John as they continued their covert conversation.

"Lexi is going to kill me! She thinks I was the one who invited Charlie."

John scoffed. "That is completely ludicrous Sam. You hate the man. Why would you invite him anywhere?"

I reeled in horror, blocking out the sound of Samantha's voice. I dashed into my dressing room leaving Astral Charlie behind to act as my eyes and ears. I shut the door just as I heard Harry blurt out, "Well hello there! Is Charlie around?"

I locked the door of my dressing room and pressed my ear up against the door trying to make out what they were saying.

The entire crew stared at one another without saying a word as Harry adjusted his belt buckle. "How did today's taping go?" There was dead silence. You could hear a pin drop until Harry cracked his neck. "Woof! I needed that." The silence continued. "What's wrong with all of you people? You look like you just saw a ghost! Do I have something in my nose?" Harry grabbed his nose and then turned around and glanced at his reflection in the on-set hair and make-up station. "Nope, handsome as ever! Damn, how do I do it?" Clapping his hands, Harry barked. "Okay! Gather around everybody. I have an announcement to make. First off, I want you all to know how much we appreciate you, which is why I'm inviting you to the hottest shindig in town!"

Astral Charlie flew over to Harry's side and watched as he passed out invitations to the entire staff. "I rented La Mystique for the night, so everybody get ready to eat, drink, and be merry while we wish Charlie a very happy birthday!"

Samantha huffed and snorted. "I knew there was a catch!"

Harry continued. "Now obviously the party isn't mandatory, but I am trying to put the finishing touches on the movie deal of Charlie's life." Harry rubbed his hands together. "So it'd be great if all of you could come by for just a little while. You can bring a date, have a few free drinks on the boss and be on your merry way. Or... you could stay for the entire event, kiss your boss's ass so that the executives see how much you love working for this show." The crowd of employees began to murmur and make cracks beneath their breath. Harry cleared his throat interrupting their chatter. "Remember, bonus time is right around the corner!" The

89

room quieted down. "Okay, so the magic starts at eight o'clock sharp and anyone who gets Charlie a gift should expect a little thicker envelope. Any questions?"

A man with a semi baldhead stepped forward. "I was just wondering who you have keeping track of the gifts because if you need a volunteer I could offer my services."

Harry scoffed. "Okay listen. I was bluffing about the thicker envelope, but like it or not Charlie is the reason we are here. It's not easy to go out there and be a total asshole day in and day out. When I met Charlie he was a sweet kid with a bruised ego and not a clue about what sells. I was the one who masterminded that bruised ego into a multi-million dollar franchise called, 'Angry Movie Guy'. What I'm trying to say is, if it wasn't for me none of you would be here right now."

Astral Charlie began to clap, but no one heard him. "Why do I even bother?" Astral Charlie whined as he rolled his eyes. Just then Samantha began to whisper to John and Astral Charlie flew over to her side to investigate. He hovered over Samantha trying to make out what she was saying.

Samantha laughed and ridiculed Harry. "Ha! Like Charlie is 'acting' like an asshole."

John turned to Samantha whispering behind the crowd of employees. "You've got to take it easy Sam. You don't want to lose your job over this. Don't you have all those student loans to pay off? Just explain to your cousin that you had nothing to do with the review and life will go on."

Samantha pouted, "Oh yeah, while the whole family thinks I'm a total bitch for working for a guy who tore my cousin's film apart! Feel my forehead John. I think I'm running a fever. I'm supposed to go to Lexi's tomorrow evening to watch the review. It'll be just a few friends and me, the backstabber! What am I going to do John? Alex has it in her head that Charlie likes her. I told Lexi he is a maniac, not to be trusted, but she told me not to worry. I can't figure out how this all happened? Charlie wasn't on the list of reviewers to see the film. I would know, because I made the list!"

John bit his lip. "Oh... that's why Alex thinks you're responsible for bringing Charlie to the film?"

Sam's face began to wrinkle. "Yes! You moron...err...I'm sorry. I didn't mean that. I'm just stressed." Samantha ran off the set with tears boiling over in her eyes.

Astral Charlie shrugged his shoulders. "Chicks!"

John held up his hand and Harry pointed to him. "Okie-dokie, you in the back, but uh, this is the last question... I got a tanning appointment."

John put his hand down and shook his head. "Never mind, it's not important."

Harry put his cowboy hat back on and clapped his hands. "Great! If nobody else has anything to say, I'll see you all Mañana! Oh! And one more thing, no rubber chickens please. I want to see something nice on the table, like maybe a new tie or a coffee mug with Charlie's name on it. Remember this could be a deal breaker folks, so let's act like we all like Charlie... just for the day, okay?"

The crowd grunted as Harry sauntered off yelling, "See you tomorrow night at eight pm sharp!"

Astral Charlie flew off as the crowd dispersed and headed for my dressing room. I pulled my ear away from the door not having a clue what was said about me, but the mere act of standing with my head pressed against the door for twenty minutes confirmed I needed therapy. I bolted out the back door of the studio to go and discuss my "feelings" with Dr. Bloom, or lack of them according to most of America.

Dr. Bloom was cheerful as always to see me. He stuck his head out into the empty waiting room and said "Be with you in ten minutes Charlie."

I nodded my head and went back to daydreaming. Over the years, I had assessed Dr. Bloom's career. I determined if Dr. Bloom could spend all day telling people what was wrong with them he must have a pretty high self-esteem yet, something didn't add up. Dr. Bloom had no wife or girlfriend to speak of and as far as I could tell he wasn't gay. Truth be told, he was practically living the same lonely existence I was living. "And, I'm coming here twice a week!" I muttered to myself as I stood up and began pacing the floors of the tiny waiting room while I imagined what it would be like if the tables were turned. I pointed my pen in the direction of where I imagined Dr. Bloom to be sitting and beckoned him to come clean. "Let's get down to business Dr. Bloom. We both know your hiding something. It's written all over your face. I sincerely hoped after years of listening to your patients empty their dirty laundry that you would have gotten up the courage to let the cat out of the bag, but I can see that was just to much too ask for? Well, the gig is up. It's time to come clean!" I sat down and picked up a Vanity Fair magazine with Tom Cruise on the cover. "I see how it is. You want to play hardball? All right, we'll do this your way. Where did we last leave off?" I flipped through the pages of the Vanity Fair, whispering to myself. "Aw! Yes, here it is... you were saying that your mother was a very domineering woman who hated that you dressed better than she did?" I looked up and stared out into the empty office. "That's not you?" I said, as I casually flipped a page of the magazine turning to a story of Liza Minnelli. "Of course not. I must have confused with another patient of mine." I drew a mustache across a model's face and then tossed the magazine aside. I grabbed a GQ magazine off the stand and whispered, "Let me see... ah yes, here it is, you were saying that your father was a kleptomaniac and your mother had a severe drinking problem. Tell me about that." I felt like I was on the verge of discovering something extraordinary about Dr. Bloom, but before I could conduct a proper analysis my imaginary session came to a close.

Dr. Bloom popped his head out of his office. "Charlie, I'm ready for you."

I walked in wondering if Dr. Bloom heard me talking to myself. As always, Dr. Bloom turned over an hourglass indicating the session was to begin and then he picked up his yellow notepad.

"So, how is everything going at work Charlie?"

I looked at Dr. Bloom and for the first time in years I felt like I could trust him.

"Dr. Bloom, may I lay down on the couch?"

Dr. Bloom smiled. "Of course Charlie! Mi casa es su casa."

I stretched out on the couch and looked at Dr. Bloom.

"Are you feeling okay Charlie?"

I grinned. "Actually I feel great!"

Dr. Bloom beamed, "That's wonderful Charlie! I take it my advice worked?"

I shook my head. "You know what... I actually think it did."

Dr. Bloom crossed his legs. "Really? Do tell!"

A look of confusion swept across my face. "You sound surprised Dr. Bloom?"

Dr. Bloom's happy face changed to a serious expression. He leaned forward. "No. It's just that we haven't had a breakthrough in quite a while. I was becoming concerned with my approach towards your recovery, which is why I was trying something new.... it's called creative visualization. I imagined this method being the only thing in the world that would work for you and it did. So it seems like my job here is done."

I sat up. "Now wait a minute! Nobody said I was cured. I said I was feeling better than usual. I ran into that girl again."

Dr. Bloom looked over his wire-framed glasses. "Really?"

I gleamed with pride. "Yes, it was quite unexpected. I thought I'd made her up, but then she showed up at an independent film festival I was attending."

Dr. Bloom wrote something on his yellow pad. "What was she doing there Charlie?"

I sat up, staring at Dr. Bloom who was doodling stick figures of me lying on the couch. "I don't know? Who cares? The important thing is she's real. I'm not a total nut job like some of the quacks you have coming here."

Dr. Bloom nodded his head. "Well, that's great Charlie... so now what?"

My eyebrows rose inquisitively. "Now what? Well, now I guess I go out with her?"

Dr. Bloom uncrossed his legs. "That is great news Charlie!"

I sighed. "But she hasn't called me yet!"

Dr. Bloom smiled staring at his pendulum on his desk as it went back and forth mocking my therapeutic catharsis. "Why don't you call her Charlie? You do know it is customary for the male to call the female?"

I glared at Dr. Bloom. "I know that. Do you think I'm an absolute moron?"

I pointed at Dr. Bloom. "Don't answer that. The thing is...I would call her, but I don't have her number. I was in such a rush that I only had time to give her my business card."

Dr. Bloom's smile turned to a look of concern. "Charlie, you ran into the woman of your dreams and you didn't take the time to get her phone number?"

I rubbed my forehead. "I know what you're thinking. I'm an imbecile, a self-centered jackass, but I'm under a lot of pressure because the head of the studio is hell-bent on getting a movie deal based on my life's work."

Dr. Bloom's eyebrow's raised. "Really? And that prevented you from getting her number?"

I rubbed my forehead. "Yes, I mean no. Look, I was running late for this stupid independent film event which, apparently is the deal breaker on whether or not they officially decide to turn my ability to be a complete ass into a feature film."

Dr. Bloom yawned. "That sounds great Charlie!"

I turned to my side. "Yeah, yeah, it's wonderful."

Dr. Bloom tapped the tip of his pencil on his yellow note pad and smirked. "Tell me Charlie, what is this beauties name?"

I rubbed my temples. "Her name?"

"Yes. You did ask Cinderella her name, right?" Dr. Bloom examined my reaction.

"Actually, I haven't gotten that far yet."

Dr. Bloom scribbled a note on his pad. "Oh. I see. How far have you gotten Charlie?"

I was becoming agitated by Dr. Bloom's line of questioning.

"Look, you're starting to make me feel like I'm hallucinating again."

Dr. Bloom set his pad down. "Don't think like that Charlie. I'm simply trying to understand how you plan to go out with a woman whose name you do not know and whose number you don't have?"

I stood up irritated. "Look doc, I was just nervous and pretty much a bumbling idiot, but she exists and I managed to give her my card! She said she would call me and I believe her." I headed towards the door, but was stopped by Dr. Bloom's encouraging words.

"That's great Charlie." I turned around and Dr. Bloom continued, "Where are you going? This session isn't finished."

I glared at Dr. Bloom. "Look, I know what you're thinking."

Dr. Bloom cocked his head. "Oh yeah, what am I thinking?"

I took a deep breath. "You're thinking that it's an infatuation. But it's not. I am around beautiful women every day and they do nothing for me. She was different. She just fits. For the first time in years, I felt like I could be myself."

Dr. Bloom picked his pad back up. "You've never talked like this before Charlie, I'm surprised…tell me more." Walking back to the couch I grabbed the rubber ball from Dr. Bloom's desk and squeezed it hard searching for the right words to describe my inner emotions. "I felt like I was young again doc, like when my mother was alive!"

Dr. Bloom seemed intrigued. "How fascinating. Tell me more Charlie."

I paused. "She just had a way of making me feel important, the way my mother did when she was alive. Though my Mother was a glamorous movie star, she genuinely wanted to know what I thought. I know I was her only son and everything, but I'm not making it up when I say my mother really wanted to know my opinion."

Dr. Bloom smiled and encouraged me to get to root of my issue. "And this woman made you think of your mother Charlie?"

I shook my head no. "No, not really, she actually made me think of Jack Waters from *Lost in Her Eyes*."

Dr. Bloom squinted his eyes and then dug deeper looking for the origin of my problem. "And why is that, Charlie?"

I threw the rubber ball in the air. "I guess I always thought that somehow we are all making a movie and there has to be a leading lady, right?"

Dr. Bloom made a note. "Interesting analogy Charlie."

I threw the rubber ball in the air again and caught it. "Well, my movie never had a leading lady. And it had a pretty shitty leading man…me."

Dr. Bloom intercepted the ball as I tossed it into the air. "May I interrupt you for a minute Charlie?"

I turned and looked at Dr. Bloom. "Sure."

Dr. Bloom set the ball on the table. "You know what it sounds like to me Charlie?"

I rolled my eyes. "That I'm crazy?"

Dr. Bloom shook his head. "No. Not at all Charlie. It sounds like she made you happy just being you."

I grabbed the rubber ball again and squeezed it hard. "That's right! God, you're good! That's exactly it. Her mere presence was enough. I felt as though I could conquer the world with her!"

Dr. Bloom smiled. "I sure hope she calls Charlie." He then looked down at his watch and began rubbing it. I could tell he was ready to give me the same old speech until I interrupted him.

"You know what Doc? I think I'm going to take next week off."

Dr. Bloom questioned me. "Did I hear you correctly? You want to skip our next session?"

I was about to retract my words, but I decided against it. "That's right. I feel like something has been miraculously lifted off my shoulders."

Before I could stop him Dr. Bloom stood up and opened his big hairy arms and wrapped them around me. He said, "I feel like giving you a hug Charlie. I'm proud of you."

I stiffened at Dr. Bloom's embrace. When he finally let go of me I didn't say a word; instead I slowly backed out of his office.

On the ride home I wanted to stop for ice cream, but I didn't. "Just keep driving," I said to myself. I also had an urge to turn on the radio and listen to other people complain on Dr. W's self-help program, but I resisted. I took a deep breath and reiterated Dr. Bloom's advice to myself. "Self indulgence won't solve anything Charlie." I caught my reflection in the rearview mirror and noticed I was smiling. At that moment, I decided to drive home in complete silence. Somewhere in the silence, a brilliant idea emerged. "I'm going to go and visit my mother's gravesite."

I made a U-turn onto the expressway and headed towards Riverdale. I drove for two hours stopping only to purchase my mother some flowers. I walked into the desolate cemetery and stopped at the entrance to listen to the sound of the birds chirping. I looked up at the dwindling sun shining in the sky and knew it would be dark soon. I rushed to my mother's gravesite, unprepared for the overwhelming sense of grief that was about to engulf me. "Hi Mom. It's me, your son, Charlie. It's been a while. I uh, brought you some flowers." I set the flowers down by her tombstone and stood back so that I could read the inscription.

> Evelyn Zimmerman
> 'To a woman who had enough Love
> for the entire world.
> May you rest in peace Evelyn.'
> 1940-1976

"Wow! They really got that one right mom. You are one of a kind." A flood of tears welled up in my eyes and began to run down the side of my cheeks. "It's my birthday tomorrow Mom. I thought since you couldn't come to me I would come to you. I miss you. Nothing's been the same since you died. To be honest, my life has been miserable. I'm a fat old man who has no girlfriend, no friends and an empty feeling in the pit of my stomach. Not much to be proud of except that I became a film critic." I laughed. "Who am I kidding? I give horrible reviews that ruin people's self-esteem and even their lives at times. I'm a loser."

Backing away from the gravestone I whispered, "This isn't going the way I expected. I mean I didn't come here looking for your approval or anything. I already know what you must be thinking. How could that be my son?" I sighed. "You are so amazing and I'm, well nothing good could be said for what I've become." I set my hand on her gravestone looking to connect with her spirit. "I want you to know that it's not your fault. I mean, maybe some of it had to do with the fact that I spent my entire childhood with Aunt Hilda? But you didn't know that Dad was going to drop me off never to return again." I took a deep breath. "Good news is… I'm changing. There is a woman in my life now. She's terrific. You'd love her, actually she reminds me of you. And I'm nearly ready to quit therapy! Yeah, it's for the best. I'm going to put my money into something else. I figure my therapist's winter home has got to be paid off by now. So why not buy one of my own?" I rubbed my hands over my face trying to leave the past in the past like Dr. Bloom suggested. "Well that's it for me Mom. How about you?" I paused. There was dead silence in the cemetery until I spoke again. "They say death is easy. It's living that's hard. Is that true?" I moaned. "Never mind, you don't have to answer that. Did you see the flowers I brought you? I made sure they stuck a few of your favorites in the bunch. I remember how happy you were when your gardenias would bloom." Suddenly tears began to stream from my eyes. I could barely see, let alone speak, so I decided to cut my visit short. In between the convulsing and sobbing I tried to say my goodbyes to my mother. "I better go Mom, but I want you to know how much I love you and when I get home I'm going to watch one of your movies. I haven't done that since I was kid. Bye Mom." I ran back to my Porsche and drove home balling my eyes out.

Astral Charlie was overwhelmed with grief as well, but he felt compelled to help me face the loss of my mother. After arriving home I rummaged through a box of my mother's old tapes till I found my favorite, a romantic comedy titled, *Under the Cover's*.

I was about to play it when a little voice sounded off inside my head. "Charlie! Play *Till the End*!" I shook my head, but the voice continued. "It's time Charlie. Your mother wants you to watch it. Play *Till the End*!" Astral Charlie floated over me, screaming at the top of his lungs till I began to rummage through the cardboard box of tapes and pulled out, *Till the End*.

Returning to my bedroom, I watched, *Till the End* for the very first time. As the movie played, I kept hearing a voice saying, "It's okay Charlie, nobody can hear you. Just let it out!"

And I did. I wailed at the top of my lungs wishing I could be a baby again, so that my mother could hold me in her arms.

The following morning I woke up earlier than usual and made a phone call to a guy I knew in London. I spent hours on the phone going over the arrangements to play rare never been seen footage from *Till the End*. I knew it was time for me to start over and to do that I needed to say goodbye to my mother for real this time. After the phone call ended I passed out on the couch, worn out from my great feat of courage. I slept right through my six and seven a.m. alarm clock alert. I had never missed a taping of the show and today would be no different. Luckily, I had taken the day off from berating Hollywood in hopes of celebrating my birthday. What a joke.

Astral Charlie hovered over me hoping I would wake up so he could pester me about my assistant Samantha's weird behavior, but I was passed out cold. Hours passed before Astral Charlie got up the nerve to venture out on his own. He rushed over to my assistant Samantha's home to determine why her panties were in such a bunch. He knew the slightest disturbance from an outsider might disrupt my new found sense of self and he wanted to keep me out of therapy for good.

RE-BIRTH

Chapter Six

Coincidentally, Samantha had also planned to stay home from work. Astral Charlie floated over Samantha's bed waiting for her to awake. Her alarm clock blared for the tenth time startling Samantha out of her deep lethargic slumber. She rolled over in her queen size orthopedic bed and began to bang on top of her blaring Sony alarm clock, nearly breaking it. Still half asleep, Samantha reached for her silver wire framed glasses and iPhone off the nightstand and dialed John's number at the studio. His phone went straight to voicemail.

"Hi John, this is Sam. I thought you'd like to know that I'm not going to work today because I'm busy having a mental break down! And I know what you're thinking, "It's not that big of a deal, but it is. My cousin Lexi put her entire life savings into that film and I watched Charlie rip it apart without blinking an eye."

Samantha screamed and then hung up the phone. "He is officially a monster!" Samantha dialed her supervisor at the studio. The phone rang, "Hello? Achoo! Yes sir, it's Samantha. I'm terribly sorry sir, but I feel awful. Achoo! Achoo! Yes, thank you, I will take care of myself. No... No... I don't think it's the flu.

I should be able to come in to work tomorrow. Okay, thank you. Achoo!" Samantha hung up the phone and began muttering profanities out loud; she was completely unaware of Astral Charlie's presence. "There is no way in hell I am going to celebrate that evil maggot's birthday. Besides, after my cousin watches Charlie's review I'll probably be busy scraping her off of the pavement." Sam walked to her closet and picked out a dark blue Club Monaco tennis dress from her closet and slipped on a pair of blue and white Nike flip-flops. She didn't bother with her hair; instead she tied it back into a ponytail and headed to the East Village.

All the while, I remained fast asleep at home as Astral Charlie flew close behind Samantha, glued to her every move. Astral Charlie felt like Sherlock Holmes as he followed Samantha into an old world style Italian café named Veniero on east Eleventh Street. He flew around the cafe checking out all the delicious looking cookies, pies, and cakes. He stuck his finger into a piece of dark chocolate pie on the shelf.

"Mm, delicious!"

Meanwhile, Samantha stood in an abnormally long line waiting to pick up a triple layered cake she had ordered for her cousin Lexi. While standing in line, her phone buzzed. Samantha looked down and read a disturbing text from John.

Text: Hey! Sorry you're "sick" but if you think you got out of Charlie's b-day, no such luck! Harry phoned the studio this morning to let us know the party is now scheduled for tomorrow at La Mystique, at 7:30 P.M.

Samantha growled at John's text and then wrote him back.

Text: You have got to be kidding me?

Samantha read the text over and over again before letting out a loud scream, "Aaaahh!!!" Looking up Sam realized a large security guard and several Veniero customers glaring at her. "Great!" Samantha sighed, as she watched the security guard walk up to her in line.

"Mam, is there a problem?"

Samantha smiled timidly as she answered the enormous Dominican security guard.

"No sir."

The security guard glanced at the angry customers in line and then reprimanded Samantha.

"Then kindly keep your voice down. You are disturbing the other customers."

Samantha faintly smiled at the guard. "Yes sir. Of course, it won't happen again. I just got an awful text from my job."

Sam turned her iPhone around to show the guard her text, but the guard seemed un-interested. He folded his arms and shook his head. "I'm not interested in reading your phone Mam. Just keep it down." Then the security guard walked back to where he was standing by the front door.

Samantha rolled her eyes. "Geeze! Since when does a bakery need security?"

The man standing in front of Samantha turned around and scoffed. "Since when do you think?" Then he cupped his ear like he had just lost his hearing.

Samantha sarcastically grinned at the flamboyant looking gentleman. "I don't know sir, but I am sure you are going to let me know."

Astral Charlie laughed; he was amused by Samantha's antics. His time away from his corporal self was turning out better than he imagined.

The man removed his hands from his ears and muttered, "You got it sister…since they started letting people like you in here!" Then he dramatically tugged on his ear lobe.

Sam rolled her eyes again. "Yes, yes, of course I'm sure I'm the reason. Now if you don't mind I was just in the middle of something." Samantha went back to texting John without apologizing for her behavior.

Text: You've got to be kidding me John! I'm going to my cousin's house tonight to watch that awful review and then tomorrow I have to show up at his birthday with a gift?

John looked at his phone and quickly wrote back.

Text: I know it sucks Samantha, but if you don't show up they might just make your life a living hell.

Astral Charlie hovered over Sam licking the chocolate pie filling off of his hands while watching Samantha ferociously text John.

Samantha laughed out loud and the people in line began to glare at her again. **Text: HA! Make my life a living hell? What do you think it is now?** Samantha hit send.

John's Text: Nobody takes his reviews seriously Sam. He's trashed every movie in the last year.

Samantha's Text: Yeah I know, but not the way he did my cousin's. A few seconds went by and John responded.

John's Text: It's probably all part of the act. He has to give it a worse review because she's a newbie in the business.

Astral Charlie stared at the text, "OH!" He finally put two and two together. "You're related to that stupid filmmaker. That's awful. You must feel awful."

Samantha walked up to the counter and gave the woman her ticket. The woman at the register grabbed her order and set a triple-layer chocolate, vanilla and strawberry marble cake down in front of her. She opened the box and read the inscription on the cake aloud. "To a true beauty... A true talent... And a true Inspiration! We love you Lexi!"

The clerk smiled and said, "Wow. That's beautiful!"

Samantha smiled at the woman and then sighed. "Yeah, I just hope she believes it."

The woman handed a Viernos brown paper bag with handles to Sam and said, "I'm sure she will.... have a good day."

Astral Charlie flew after Samantha excited about going to a party. He stuck by Samantha's side the entire day completely oblivious to how long he had been away from his corporal self. Little did Astral Charlie know that before attending the gathering he was going to have to listen to Sam moan the entire day about the review? Astral Charlie began to wish he had stayed home until he remembered I was probably sulking as well.

Truth is, I was still fast asleep. I had woken up just long enough to notice it was dark outside. I checked my watch and realized I had slept through my entire birthday, so I decided why ruin a good thing. I popped a couple of sleeping pills and stumbled up the stairs to my bed.

Samantha arrived at her cousin's Greenwich Village brownstone apartment just in time for the review to play on air. Alex opened the door with a warm smile on her face.

"Samantha, you're here. Finally! Look who it is everybody… Samantha!"

A crowd full of guests peered towards the door as Sam nervously stared back at them. Sam tried to return Lexi's warm gesture, but it was nearly impossible. She coyly entered Lexi's brownstone apartment and handed Alex the large brown bag of goodies.

Meanwhile, Astral Charlie floated near by Samantha staring at Alex in shock. He finally realized the damage he had done.

"You're her! You're my… I mean your Charlie's dream girl!"

Alex glanced inside the bag. "Wow, this is heavy. What do you have in here?" Alex looked in the bag. It was filled with alcohol. "This is way too much Sam. You shouldn't have."

Samantha realized the whole room was staring at her and began to feel uncomfortable. "Hey, what's family good for if they can't get you liquored up. Right?"

Alex took the alcohol out of the bag and set it on the counter in the dining room. "My God! You brought enough to keep me toasted for the next month."

Samantha reached into a second bag and helped Lexi take out the cake. "Yeah, I thought we might need a little something extra to celebrate all those good reviews you already received."

Alex clapped her hands. "This is so exciting! My first review on television." She put her arms around Samantha. "And it's all because of you."

Samantha pulled away from Lexi, almost dropping the gorgeous cake. "No. I'm not responsible for this."

Alex grinned at Sam and then looked over at the room full of guests. "You keep saying that Sam, but why else would he come to see my film if it wasn't for you?"

Astral Charlie began to panic. "You can't let her watch the review! Charlie will be mortified. He loves her. I love her! We love her! Please! You have to do something. He will send us back to therapy or worse a mental institution!"

Sam pulled Alex into the kitchen away from her anxious guests. "Lexi, have you ever seen Charlie's show?"

A look of guilt suddenly overcame Alex. "Just once or twice. You know I don't watch T.V. Sam."

Samantha opened a bottle of Pinot Noir and then shouted from the kitchen. "Anyone care for a glass of wine?"

Lexi peered into the living room and saw all her guest's hands in the air. "I guess that's a yes." Lexi walked back into the kitchen and began pouring the wine. She smiled at Samantha. "It certainly came as a big surprise to see him there. Are you sure you had nothing to do with it?"

Samantha shook her head "Positive!"

Just then, Lexi's black pit bull named Knock-out came running into the kitchen wagging his stubby tail. "Good boy Knock-out! Alex bent down to pet her enormous puppy on the head and continued prodding Samantha about her involvement. "I think you are being modest Sam, but I'll leave it for now. Did you know I saw him afterwards?"

Samantha's face turned white. "You did?"

Astral Charlie squealed like a pig. "You did? Where was I?" Astral Charlie began to tap his fingers on the kitchen counter. "He's keeping things from me. I knew it. Just wait till I get home. Doesn't he know we are a team?"

Lexi grinned mischievously at Sam. "Well sort of. He looked awful, like wolves had attacked him. Anyway… I tried talking to him, but he just dashed off before I could tell him I was the director. He seemed really sweet though."

Samantha dipped a piece of celery into ranch dressing and began to chomp on it. "Charlie seemed sweet?"

Lexi sipped her wine. "Ah yeah, you seem shocked? He even asked me out."

Samantha began to choke on the piece of celery she was eating and Alex tapped her on the back.

"Samantha, are you alright?"

Samantha coughed louder and then gasped for air while replying to Samantha. "Yeah. I'm fine! I just got a little celery caught in my throat."

Alex handed Samantha a glass of water. "Here drink this!" Then Alex picked up her glass of wine and glanced down at her watch. "Oh my God! Would you look at the time? My first review is about to air! Samantha, can you please bring the appetizers into the living room? I'll be right back. I'm so nervous that I've used the little girls room like a dozen times today."

Samantha picked up the platter of vegetarian snacks and set them on the coffee table next to a collection of Vogue magazines. She glanced up at Alex's guests and whispered, "Cover me," as she bent down to disconnect the 36' inch flat screen Sony plasma television from the cable box.

Astral Charlie watched Sam in anticipation. "She's actually going to stop this thing from happening. We need to give this girl a raise."

Sam fiddled with the T.V. until Bunny; a long time friend of Lexi's jumped up from the couch and began questioning Sam's peculiar motives.

"Just what do you think you are doing?"

Wild-eyed from not sleeping, Sam snapped at Bunny. "I'm trying to save my cousin from an utterly humiliating situation. So just do me a favor and play along. Okay!?"

Bunny shrugged her shoulders and then sat back down on the couch. "Okay, if you say so."

A few guests stood in the threshold of the living room watching for Alex. "Psst, she's coming!"

Samantha dashed back to the couch as Alex entered the living room beaming from ear to ear. The entire living room stared at Lexi uncomfortably.

"You guys are so quiet, it's making me nervous. This is supposed to be a celebration!" Alex turned on the television, but there was nothing but static. "Oh no! There is no way I forgot to pay for Time Warner?" Alex turned the channel, but it was the same thing on every station.

Astral Charlie flew in front of the T.V. trying to help. He thought his etheric body might disturb the frequency and cause Alex's cable box to glitch, but no such luck!

"This is awful!" Sam said, "I can't believe we're going to miss your review!"

Alex began to look around the T.V. spotting the loose wire. "It's okay Sam. I found it. Knock-out probably banged it loose." Alex re-hooked the loose wire. "Presto! See, it's working again."

Samantha cleared her throat. "Wow! You fixed it!"

Alex smiled. "What can I say? You work on a movie set long enough and you pick up a few good things."

Lexi gave her cousin a big hug and then joined her guests on her long red velvet antique couch. Samantha was finally ready to deliver the bad news. "Lexi I have to tell you something…"

Samantha interrupted her. "Can't it wait Samantha? The review is about to begin."

Astral Charlie turned and saw his own face on the screen and he felt like puking. "Oh my God, why do I do these things? Maybe Charlie's right. Maybe we do need to be in therapy?"

Lexi turned to Sam and whispered, "He looks so handsome on screen."

Samantha's jaw dropped in horror as the review of Alex's film began.

Astral Charlie moaned loudly. "We're doomed!"

The review played on the T.V. screen. "It's another week and yet another two hours of my life that I'll never be able to get back. It's film festival season so I thought I'd get out there and see what some of the indie filmmakers had to offer…"

The review seemed to last a lifetime. When it ended Sam stood up with the other pensive guests. Sam approached Lexi. "Soooo! Talk with you tomorrow Lexi?"

Alex didn't budge. She just sat their stoned face, not saying a word. Samantha scurried to the front door with the rest of the guests. Once all the guests were out the door she turned to her cousin. "I'm so sorry Alex. I wanted to tell you, but you were so excited."

Alex shook her head. "It's not your fault Sam."

Sam tried to shut the door behind her, but was stopped by one of Lexi's oldest friends. "Don't sweat it Alex, this guy is a total prick. Call you tomorrow?"

Alex mumbled, "Sure thing." Then she slammed the door shut.

TRIAL & ERROR

Chapter Seven

The following morning I woke up feeling like I had been run over by a semi-truck. I held my head, wincing in pain wondering why I felt like I had a hangover. I thought it might be my sleeping pills; I had no idea it was because Astral Charlie had discovered my new fuck up and had decided to play God. With limited resources, Astral Charlie elected to send me visions of being hooked up with one starry-eyed bimbo after the next while I slept. His goal was to appeal to my subconscious.

"You are rich and successful Charlie! Chicks dig that crap! You could easily have a life of mind-boggling sex with woman who would literally bend over backwards to make you happy!"

Astral Charlie hoped that by morning time I would be ready to throw in the towel on all the love crap that had suddenly consumed me, but his desperate attempts were unsuccessful. It seemed that even my subconscious understood that no matter how rich and famous I became I would never enjoy a life of meaningless sex with gorgeous woman. I just didn't have it in me, like some men did.

I sat up in bed and pondered over what had transpired in the last few days of my life. I finally felt like I had learned to accept my mother's death. What I hadn't learned to let go of was how my father mistreated me. I slid out of bed and looked out the window at my gorgeous Central Park view. I smiled. It doesn't matter I thought to myself. So what if my father went out and humped every young woman he met after my mother died. C'est la vie to the family heirlooms he hocked during his drinking and gambling phase. It's only priceless memorabilia. Sure it wasn't fair, but life isn't fair.

I gazed at my reflection in the mirror noticing that something about me appeared different. I looked around the bathroom for the scale. Maybe I lost weight? I thought, as I hopped on the scale and anxiously watched the needle jump to 220lbs. "I did lose weight!" I exclaimed. "How the hell did that happen?" Just then, the doorbell rang. I ran down the stairs of my condo and peeked through the peephole. A stunning woman in a tan trench coat stood at my front door. Astral Charlie also peeked through the peephole. He was just as stunned, as I was to see the foxy female standing outside. For a second, Astral Charlie actually thought he was responsible for her presence.

He screamed. "It worked!"

I slowly opened the door and the woman in the long tan trench coat seductively began to coo in my ear.

"Harry Pubei wanted me to stop by and wish a certain naughty boy a very happy birthday."

The sexy female opened her coat and revealed her half naked body. She was wearing black lacy lingerie with thigh-high stockings attached to a garter belt. She began to sing happy birthday to me breathlessly like Marilyn Monroe until I shut the door in her face.

Astral Charlie yelped, "What are you doing? That was your chance to put this broad behind us Charlie. Open the door! You're making a mistake. Charlie!"

I moped into the kitchen and poured myself a cup a coffee while listening to the floozy bang on my front door.

"What are you gay?" She screamed.

I made a phone call to Harry and left him a message. "Thanks for the bimbo, but my birthday was yesterday!"

I hung up the phone and sat down at the kitchen table. I grinned as I sipped my mug of coffee. As odd as it may seem it felt really good to slam the door on that escort's face. Most men in my shoes would have let her in and ravaged her for breakfast. Maybe I'm not such an asshole after all? I thought to myself. Maybe it's all Harry's influence? I began to reminisce about the time Harry entered my life. Eventually I fell fast asleep at the table with the mug of coffee still in my hand.

I traveled back in time to when I was fresh out of college, desperate and avoiding my overbearing father's phone calls. My phone rang. I stared at my father's name on the caller id. I knew if I didn't answer the phone soon Ray would show up at my front door. "Hello."

My father yelled, "Charlie? Where the hell have you been? I've been calling you for weeks. Listen up! Meet me tomorrow at Butcbinder's on the Upper East Side at eight o'clock sharp!"

I muttered, "Tomorrow? Tomorrow might not be so good for me Ray. I have to…"

My father cut me off. "Oh no you don't! Tomorrow is just fine for you Charlie. And wear that suit I bought you. I got a buddy I want you to meet. It's time for you to get a real job!"

I hung up the phone. "Damn it!"

The following day I showed up at Butchbinder's dressed in the best suit I had in my closet, which was ripped and had a stain on it. I had outgrown the suit my father sent me years ago and he knew it. Ray had set up a dinner at a fancy restaurant and invited a guy he barely knew from a T.V. station to come and meet me.

I moped into the fancy restaurant. "Hey dad."

Ray looked at me with disdain. "What are you waiting for a written invitation? Sit down already."

I sat down and he started in on me right away. "Listen Charlie, you've given this movie critique thing a shot. It's been years and you've done squat with it. It's time for you to stop living off me. I'm cutting you off!"

I turned to my father searching for a decent rebuttal. "You can't. I've almost lined up a job!"

Ray slammed his fist on the table. "I've heard this shtick before! Enough is enough Charlie. I got this guy coming to meet you. His name is Harry Pucbei, he is a big time television producer who is setting up shop here."

I stopped my father. "Wait a second, your friend's name is Harry Pubes." I began to laugh.

"It's pronounced Pue…bays, you smart ass."

I rolled my eyes. "Still, I don't know a thing about television Dad."

My father retorted. "You don't know anything about anything. Look Charlie, the ride is over. I've got Yasmine to think about and besides you're twenty-seven for Christ's sakes. You need to start thinking about your future and start stocking some money away."

I looked at him with disdain and began to laugh in his face. "Isn't Yasmine twenty-seven?"

Ray smirked. "Actually she's twenty-five and has the ass of a nineteen year old, but that's none of your damn business son. I told you this movie critic thing was a waste of time. Why don't you stick to what you know…writing people's obituaries?"

I began to lose all control. I hysterically burst out laughing as I watched Ray's veins bulge from his neck and his face turn bright red with scorn

"Stop being obnoxious you little twerp! It's not like you're writing anything else."

I got up and slammed my hand on the table. "I'll get a job, but it's not going to be from one of your friends."

Ray snickered to himself. "Why not genius?"

I took a few steps back from the table. "I'll tell you why not, because they're all affected jackasses with zero integrity. I've got to go. You enjoy your dinner, Dad."

I barged out of the restaurant and ran smack dab into Harry. Harry looked up at me from under his cowboy hat as I stammered, "I'm ss…ss… so sorry man."

Harry tipped his hat at me. "No problemo my friend. Go right ahead." Harry moved out of my way and I rushed off in a huff. That was the night everything changed for me.

As I drifted deeper into my past I searched for the reasons why I had allowed Harry to take over my life. I tried to make sense of it all. I squeezed my eyes shut as I drooled on the kitchen table willing myself to examine the events that had occurred years ago.

It was the morning after my little visit with my father and I was more desperate than ever to find work. I picked up the phone and dialed the New York Inquisitor with conviction. "Enough of this Mr. nice guy stuff! I've got to be cutthroat and vicious. My future depends on it!" The phone rang. "Pick it up! Come on. Pick it up already!"

The bubbly receptionist from the New York Inquisitor answered the phone. "Good afternoon. Thank you for calling the New York Inquisitor. Kelly speaking. How can I..."

I blurted out. "It's Charlie Zimmerman! Don't hang up on me Kelly!"

Kelly sighed. "Charlie? I thought I told you to stop calling here. There is nothing I can do for you. Mr. Johnson is not interested."

I shrieked. "But I have something important to say. New York Inquisitor needs what I have to offer."

Kelly took a deep breath. "I can't help you Charlie."

I slammed the stapler down on my desk and questioned Kelly like she was being cross-examined by a high-powered defense attorney. "You can't help me Kelly or you won't help me? Which is it? Because I'm a great writer and if there is one thing I know, it's the movies! So why don't you give me a shot already? Think of it this way. If you get me a job I'll stop calling! Doesn't that sound appealing to you?"

Kelly huffed, "Yes Charlie it does but…"

I pleaded with her. "Kelly, please!"

Kelly pulled the phone away from her ear. "Fine! Hold on a minute. Mr. Johnson just walked in. I'll see what I can do."

At that moment I expected to hear the same God-awful hold music I had heard a million times before, but instead I heard Kelly speaking to Mr. Johnson. "Charlie Zimmerman is on the phone again Mr. Johnson."

Mr. Johnson is a tall light skin African American man known for wearing state of the art well-tailored Italian suits. I could hear him crystal clear. "Zimmerman? Lord! I've had hemorrhoids that have been less painful and have gone away quicker than him."

I looked at my reflection in my cracked mirror and squealed, "That's ludicrous."

I imagined Kelly twirling her curly black hair between her manicured fingernails as she giggled. "I know. Tell me about it Mr. Johnson. I have to speak to him at least twice a week. He just doesn't give up." There was dead silence and then Kelly piped up in her perky thick Italian accent, which made me want to puke even in my sleep. "I could keep him on hold like I always do and then tell him we don't have anything?"

I gasped at Kelly's painful words and then silently screamed at the phone. "You asshole!"

Finally, Mr. Johnson responded, "No. I feel sort of sorry for the guy. All right, you know what? Give him Roller Baby on spec. I've got someone else covering it anyway."

Kelly pressed the hold button and spoke, "Charlie!" I didn't respond. "Charlie, you there?"

Moments later I replied, "Yeah, I'm here Kelly. What's the verdict?" My voice had changed. I no longer sounded desperate, but unemotional and cold. I could tell it disturbed Kelly.

"Well anyways, I talked with Mr. Johnson and he's willing to let you write a review for *Roller Baby* on spec. Isn't that great?"

I held my middle finger up to the phone. "Oh yeah, that's great Kelly! You tell Mr. Johnson, I won't let him down. Thanks again. You're the best." I slammed down the receiver and I went to the cheapest bar I knew to get plastered. Then I headed to the theatre to watch, *Roller Baby.* After it was over, I stumbled back to my apartment obliterated from drinking whiskey and wrote the worst review of my life. I used all the bottled up anger and frustration I had inside from the world for pushing me aside out on, *Roller Baby*. I finished the review and bellowed. "I am the greatest!!!"

That same night I went to the Inquisitor and slid the review under the door. I wanted it in the next day's paper printed for everyone to see even if it meant I would never write another review in my life. After dropping the review off I went back home and put on *Lost in Her Eyes,* for the millionth time. I was still hammered when I passed out and woke up in my dreams as Jack Waters.

I walked into the empty nightclub wearing a classic tan wool suit and fedora to match. I stood by the huge red upholstered doors and admired all that I had accomplished. The bartender was hard at work wiping down the mahogany bar. The waitress was lighting the candles on the tabletop to set the mood, while the band rehearsed their opening act. I grabbed the reservation list off the counter and made a few phone calls. Someone named Jimmy and Rick wanted to book the club for a party. I made them both an exclusive reservation and before I knew it the entire nightclub was packed with people drinking, dancing and having a swell time.

There I was, singing an original ballad I'd written, *To Have and To Hold*, accompanied by my trusted friend and pianist, Billie Coleman when she walked in. The minute I laid eyes on her I knew my whole world was about to flip upside down. From the stage, I could see that her beauty was un-like any other woman. I strolled to the back of the bar and slid up to her tipping my fedora.

"What can I do you for?"

She turned around and batted her big brown eyes.

"I'm looking for a job and the bartender told me you're the man of the house."

I smiled, "That's correct. What kind of work are you looking for sweetheart? I've got all the bartenders I need and the cigar lounge doesn't open till fall."

Edie set her evening clutch on the bar. "I don't tend bar and I prefer not to be around smoke."

I scratched my head, "Well then what kind of work are you looking for sweetheart?"

Edie batted her eyes. "Isn't it obvious." She said, in a sultry voice as she slipped off her overcoat; I almost fell over at the sight of her in a long sparkling ruby red evening gown cut as low in the front as it was in the back. "I'm a singer."

I took one look at her in that dress and I needed to order a drink. I offered her one as well. "Can I buy you a drink? I'm having a scotch on the rocks."

I glanced over at her as I motioned for the bartender, but she stood there shaking her finger back and fourth. "Heaven's no. I could never drink before I perform."

I smirked, "Well in that case we better get you on stage." I took her by the arm and walked her to the front of the nightclub. As I walked her up the stairs I realized I didn't catch her name. I leaned in close to her and whispered in her ear. "How should I introduce you?"

She gazed into my eyes and seductively whispered, "You can just tell them that I'm one of your new acts and that I'll be performing here on a regular basis. I'll take care of the rest."

I was mesmerized by her every move. I walked right up to the microphone and did as she requested. "Now coming to the stage is a lovely new act." Edie sauntered up beside me and whispered her name into my ear. "Put your hands together for Miss Edie Greene."

I sat back and listened to her sing a song I'd never heard before. I was glued to my seat the minute she grabbed the microphone and didn't let go until she stopped singing the last word of a three-song act. When she finished there was a round of applause in the club like I had never witnessed before. The audience stood up and cheered enthusiastically. I wasn't sure if it was because of her singing or because of the way she swayed in that dress. Either way she was amazing; I hired her on the spot.

Still fast asleep, dreaming in my up-town condo, I tried to refocus my dream. I had been side tracked by Jack and Edie when what I really needed to know was how I got myself mixed up with Harry in the first place. I squeezed my eyes shut and forced myself to recall my first encounter with Harry. It came to me in my dream, just like it had happened yesterday. I woke up in my Little Italy apartment muttering to myself about Jack Waters.

"This kind of stuff only happens in the movies and in my dreams."

Crash! I fell off the couch and into a pile of dirty laundry. My head was pounding and the room was spinning. Through blurred vision I saw a man walk into my living room.

"Hello? Charlie?"

The man looked around my apartment with total disdain. It was an utter disaster. It smelled of dirty old socks and rotten food. The man called out. "Charlie! Wake up, for crying out loud!" He had a hot copy of the NY Inquisitor in his hand and began to read out loud. "Let's not kid ourselves folks. *Roller Baby* is a host to all, that plagues cinema. With hardly any plot to speak of this tedious display of clichés left me praying to be whacked over the head like a baby seal and taken out of my misery."

I stared at the man standing in front of me and thought. Who is this guy? He looks vaguely familiar. I tried to get up off the floor and say something intelligent, but my thoughts were running wild and my head felt like it was splitting open so I slurred a four-letter word instead. "F@!K!" I rubbed my head and tried to clear my thoughts.

The man continued to read my review aloud. "Where did all the good ideas go? One thing is for certain none of them went into *Roller Baby*. Lightly educated sheep have more depth than to rely on scantily clad women on roller skates as a foundation for a plot. But sadly, those sheep do not run Hollywood." The man rubbed his five o'clock shadow looking at me for some sort of reaction, but when I didn't respond he continued. "If I were...."

I sprung up from the couch and grabbed the newspaper out of his hand. A huge smile crossed my face. "Holy shit! The Inquisitor printed it! They actually published it!" I grabbed my head, feeling dizzy.

Harry grabbed me just as I fell back onto the couch. "Hold on partner. I've gotcha."

I held my head. "This is awful. I can't believe they printed this awful review?"

It was then that I realized I hadn't addressed the strange cowboy in my apartment. I sprang to my feet and lifted one foot into the air like I'd seen in a thousand Bruce Lee Kung Fu movies. I screamed. "Surrender this instance and I'll let you live, but put up a fight and you'll be sure to see your grave!"

The man took one look at me and busted out laughing. "You crack me up boy. You're a real piece of work, just like your pops said. Relax, will ya? The name is Harry Puebes."

126

I smirked. "What did you just say?" I mocked him like an adolescent teenager. "Harry Pubes?"

Harry faced turned red. "Listen up, I'm only going to say this once. It's pronounced Puebay. It's French."

I stared at him in his tight jeans and cowboy hat and said, "You're French?"

Harry took off his hat revealing his shiny baldhead. "Let's move on, shall we? Do you mind if I sit down?" Harry pensively eyes me as he sat on the edge of the couch.

"What do you want?" I said, still holding the Bruce Lee crane position.

Harry shook his head. "Listen you seem upset, which is understandable considering your circumstances." He looked around at my shit hole apartment and shook his head in disbelief. "But hey, not to worry. Harry is here to save the day!" Harry smiled and then patted the edge of my filthy couch urging me to let go of my ridiculous stance. I keeled over onto the couch just before my legs gave out.

I looked up at Harry defeated. "Did my father send you here to say, I told you so! Or is it to remind me of how big of a failure I am?"

Harry grabbed the review from my hands and held it up. "Failure? They ran your review, didn't they? That's a taste of success! This is brilliant."

I responded, with a distinct sound of distrust in my voice. "Really? You really think so? Then you should check these out!" I ran to the shelf and grabbed a huge binder and handed it to Harry.

Harry flipped through my reviews. "You're a real go-getter kid. I can see that, but this is more along the lines of what I'm looking for." Harry shook the Inquisitor and then set the binder on the floor. "We need something to get their blood boiling Charlie. Something to get them fired up. We need a gimmick. Something to set you apart from everyone else." Harry stared off in space, lost in his own thoughts.

I eyed him wearily, concerned about what he might be thinking. He shot up like a bolt of lightning and slapped me on the back sending me flying off the couch.

"I've got it!"

"What? What is it?" I said, coughing from the blow to my back.

Harry stood over me. "Let me tell you something kid. Movie reviewers are a dime a dozen out there. You can't swing at a dead horse without hitting one. Everyone is a critic, nowadays!"

I was confused. "Huh?"

Harry shook his head. "Never mind. Listen, the point is you have to stand out. You need a public persona."

I looked worried. "A persona?"

Harry huffed, "Yes, Charlie! No one wants to hear some dumb chump's opinion. I hear a bad review and I go out and see the damn picture anyway, just to see for myself."

I winced. "Sure but…."

Harry looked annoyed. "But nothing Charlie. You have to be more than that. Be entertaining. Give them spice. Like what you wrote here. Now THAT had some piss 'n' vinegar to it." Harry continued, "And your name…"

I snapped at Harry. "What about my name?"

Harry snorted. "It has to go. It sounds Yiddish!"

I looked at him confused. "Yiddish? Wait a second. You're talking about my name with a last name like Pubes!"

Harry gave me a hard smack sending me back to the floor. "What did I tell you about that? Now let's concentrate!" Harry's face was red from anger. "Zimmerman doesn't pop! He does your taxes for Christ Sakes or tailors your suits. Charlie Zimmerman plays it safe."

I was dumbfounded. "Huh?"

Harry shot me a look of disdain. "Come on Charlie! Get with the program!"

I held my hand up over my head, protecting myself from Harry. "I guess you're right."

Harry smiled. "Good. Now we're on the same page. What's your mother's maiden name?"

"Gobney," I replied.

Harry tapped his finger on the Inquisitor. "Gobney?"

"Yes, Evelyn Gobney," I said, accentuating each syllable in her name slowly and clearly to get under Harry's skin.

Harry paced the room ignoring my sarcastic remark. "Interesting…I've got it!" Harry shouted, "You'll use your mother's name."

I questioned Harry's judgment. "Charlie Gobney?"

Harry shook his head. "No her first name."

I replied, "Charlie Evelyn?"

Harry looked anxious. "No, but close. From now on you'll be known as Charlie, "The Snake" Evans. Let's hear you make that snake sound!"

I tried to act like a snake slithering.

Harry rolled his eyes. "I didn't say act like a snake, I said sound like a snake!"

I apprehensively shook my head. "Crackers, that's just Crackers!"

I was still fast asleep at the kitchen table in my up-town condo when I turned my head over into a large puddle of drool. The cool wet saliva seeped inside my earlobe and I jerked in my sleep, knocking my coffee mug off the table and onto my foot. I jolted to attention as the porcelain mug hit my foot sending a severe shooting pain up the side of my body. "Damnit!"

I looked around my expensive condo, holding onto my aching wet foot. I sighed aloud. "It's true! Harry had created my persona, but it was I who had surrendered to his desire to turn my broke ass into the *Angry Movie Guy.*"

Walking up the stairs of my condo I felt woozy. I stumbled into my bathroom to get ready for the next taping of *Angry Movie Guy*. I pulled out a bottle of Xanax from my medicine cabinet, which I had lifted from Harry's office and had been popping like candy. I took the Xanax to calm my nerves, but a side effect was hallucinations. I looked into the mirror and saw a glowing figure hovering over me. Astral Charlie was levitating above me like a spirit.

"When are you going to trust me Charlie? It's just a job. You can quit any time. You have your whole life ahead of you. You're rich, you're smart and you're good looking." Astral Charlie looked at his own reflection in the mirror. I was at least fifty pounds overweight. "Oh brother!" Astral Charlie huffed. "So you're a little over weight, nothing a little Jenny Craig can't take care of. Right buddy? And remember, you're still rich, smart and you've got a full head of hair! Let's put all this Harry stuff behind us and start fresh! When you go into work today tell Harry you quit. Go on... practice it."

Astral Charlie knew I was in for a rude awakening. The woman of my dreams was never going to call me back. My assistant Samantha was probably going to quit and everything I had worked so hard for was turning into one big waste of time. I stared at myself in the bathroom mirror irked by having to go into the station.

I practiced quitting. "Harry I know we've worked together a long time and you made me into the self-righteous superstar I am today, but I quit!"

Astral Charlie began to clap. "That's right Charlie. Now walk out of the office. Go on, practice it Charlie. Walk out of the office."

I turned towards the bathroom door.

"That's it!" Astral Charlie encouraged me. "No matter what he says, you've had enough!" Astral Charlie yelled, "Leave now!"

I was about to exit the bathroom when I slipped and hit my head on the toilet bowl.

Astral Charlie flew over me screaming my name. "Charlie! Charlie!"

It was of no use; I was knocked unconscious. Two hours went by with Astral Charlie yelling my name out before I finally woke up. "You're alive Charlie! I thought you were a goner there for a minute."

I tried to get up off the floor, but I was too dizzy to stand. I held my head and winced in pain. Astral Charlie was sweating from the guilt of instigating my own pain and suffering.

"Look Charlie, I don't like to be the bearer of bad news, but you're several hours late for work and you've got a huge bump on your forehead."

I pulled my phone out of my pocket. I had twenty-two missed phone calls. I hit the call button.

Harry answered the phone. "Charlie! Where the hell are you?"

I stammered, "Harry, its Charlie."

Harry barked, "I know who it is! Where the hell are you?"

I looked around my bathroom. "Currently, I'm lying on the floor of my bathroom with a huge lump on my head."

Harry ignored my words. "You missed the taping of the show!"

"I know I did Harry. I'm sorry."

Harry responded sympathetically. "Don't be sorry Charlie."

I pulled the phone away from my ear in disbelief. "Don't be sorry?"

Harry exclaimed, "You got hit, right?"

I held my head. "Yeah."

"By whom?" Harry asked.

I stared at my bathroom door and then down at my toilet bowl. "By a door... I walked into a door Harry and knocked myself unconscious."

Harry was silent. I thought he might have hung up on me till he sarcastically blurted into the phone. "Good God Charlie! Well don't tell anyone that. You're going to make it out tonight, right?"

I sat up quickly and bumped my head on an open wooden cabinet. "Ow! Crap! Yes, of course I'm coming Harry."

Harry let out a sigh of relief. "Good. Remember we're aiming to impress these suits, so put some ice on that head of yours and pop some Excedrin." Harry hung up without even saying goodbye.

I looked down at my watch. "I still have enough time to make it to the studio. They can't have left already." I stood up holding my pounding head. "I'll just pop by the studio for a few minutes to apologize for not showing up for today's taping." I cringed at the thought of apologizing to my staff, but I knew my screw up was going to cause problems in our already intense shooting schedule.

Astral Charlie seemed relieved as he watched me stand up, until he remembered that I had no clue that I had ripped the film apart of a woman I'd fallen madly in love with. As he watched me stumble around my bedroom trying to get dressed he knew he had to do something to help me. He flew out of my bedroom like a superhero, ready to save the day.

Meanwhile, Harry was frantically trying to prepare for my surprise birthday party at La Mystique. My coworkers later told me that Harry oversaw all the preparations like a tyrant. He was barking orders at the staff as he watched dozens of balloons pour into the French restaurant. As far as Harry was concerned today was the day he was going to seal the deal on my movie contract and nothing could go wrong. *Angry Movie Guy* was going to be in theaters all across North America, even if it killed me.

CONQUEST

Chapter Eight

When Astral Charlie arrived at Alex's house it was too late. Alex was clearly inebriated and the thin line between good and evil had blurred into one straight line headed for trouble. Alex sat on her bedroom floor mumbling to herself as she continued to get hammered on the supplies Sam had given her the day before. Astral Charlie watched Alex in disbelief as she pulled a gun out from behind her bed and pointed it at the mirror.

"Charlie, you ruined my life and my film with your awful review. Prepare to die." Alex pulled the trigger on the gun and water came out. "Bang! Bang! You're dead Angry Movie Guy." Lexi stared at herself in the mirror and for a moment she appeared calm, until her phone began to ring. She hit the decline button.

Astral Charlie peered at the blinking red light on her phone. Lexi had fifteen missed calls from Gary, the producer of her film and eleven messages, which were most likely friends of hers begging her not to do something stupid. Alex picked up her phone and dialed Samantha's number as Astral Charlie tried to reason with her.

"She's not going to be able to speak with you Alex. Why don't you hang up the phone and take a cold shower?"

The phone rang and rang. Finally Samantha answered.

"Hello?"

Lexi screamed into the phone trying to be heard over the noise coming from the T.V. studio. "Where is he?"

Samantha hesitated before replying. "Alex is that you? I can barely hear you."

Lexi slurred her words. "Tell me where he is Sam! I need to speak with him!"

Alex nervously responded. "He's not here today Lexi."

Lexi scoffed. "Bullshit!"

Astral Charlie flew up to the phone and implored Alex to listen. "She's telling you the truth! We're not there. How could Charlie be at the studio, when I'm right here with you? Think about it Lexi?" Astral Charlie felt awful. He knew Samantha was devastated by what Charlie had done and he felt responsible. On top of that, Astral Charlie knew this was the busiest time of day for Samantha.

Samantha implored Lexi to calm down. "You need to calm down Lexi!"

Lexi screamed, "Don't tell me to calm down! I'm just getting started!"

Samantha put Lexi on hold. "Hold on a minute Lexi, I need to move somewhere quiet" Lexi paced the floor of her bedroom waiting for Samantha to return. Seconds later, Sam came back on the line; her voice was audible. "I'm telling you the truth Lexi. Charlie didn't show up for today's taping."

Lexi screamed into the receiver. "You're lying!"

Sam retorted. "I'm not lying! I swear I'm not!"

Alex stared into her bathroom mirror holding up the plastic gun. "I'm only going to ask this question one more time Samantha. Where is he?"

Astral Charlie was sweating bullets. "Why won't you listen to her? I'm not there!"

Unbeknownst to Astral Charlie, I was about to arrive at the studio making this phone call a lot more interesting. I rushed into the studio, surprising everyone as I began to apologize for my absence. As I was making my most heart felt apology to the director I spotted Samantha out of the corner of my eye. She was crouching in the bend of the room.

Sam lowered her voice. "No one takes him serious Alex."

Alex slurred her words as she poured herself another drink. "Well they shouldn't. He's a hack! He's a joke. A sad, bad joke!"

Sam sounded desperate. "So then just forget it Alex. It's not worth it."

Alex snapped. "Under normal circumstances Sam I would agree with you, but this is different. He destroyed my life's work."

Sam growled. "Errr! I told you he does it to everyone Alex."

Alex put the toy gun in her purse. "That is exactly why I need to set some things straight with that misogynistic bastard. He can't trash someone's life's work and think its all shits and giggles. He's got to know there are consequences for his actions Lexi."

Sam whispered into the phone. "Trust me Lexi, he doesn't care."

Alex picked up her glass of bourbon. "You know what…that is all the more reason for me to have a little shit chat with him. Now please Sam, just tell me where he is!"

Samantha took a deep breath. "I wish I could Lexi, but I haven't seen him all day."

A moment later I walked up to Samantha and stood behind her, peering over her shoulder. I cleared my throat and Samantha turned around and nearly lost it at the sight of me. Her face went pale, like she just saw a ghost. "Just a minute Alex."

Samantha covered the phone with her hand. "Is there something I can help you with Charlie?"

I bent down on one knee. "What cha' doing?" I said, to Sam with a boyish smile on my face.

Sam fiddled with a broken light switch. "I'm just trying to fix this light switch."

"Oh really?" I said, as I watched Samantha's face twitch.

"Do you need something Charlie?"

I shook my head, amused by her nervous behavior. "No, I said. I just wanted to say sorry for not making it in for today's taping."

Samantha legs began to shake from crouching in the corner. "You're sorry?"

"Yeah," I said, "for not making it in earlier today."

Samantha smiled. "Okay. Now if you'll excuse me Charlie. I'm just on the phone with the electrician." Sam held up her iPhone so that I could see.

I began to back away, embarrassed because I suddenly realized I hadn't removed the bandage from my forehead. I covered my brow. "Sure. No problem. Talk to you later Samantha."

Samantha removed her hand from the receiver. "Alex are you still there?"

Alex slurred her words. "I told you I'm not going anywhere until you tell me where he is Sam."

Sam screamed. "How many times do I have to tell you Lexi, I haven't heard or seen from him all day!"

Alex took a sip of her bourbon. "I think you're lying Sam."

Samantha was about to drive her point home, but before she could a hapless new production assistant, whose name I never bothered to learn screamed from across the empty studio.

"Well, well, if it isn't the birthday boy! I got your first drink tonight Charlie at La Mystique."

Lexi muttered, "The birthday boy?"

Astral Charlie gasped at the sound of my voice.

"Sure thing," I said, giving the new PA the thumbs up as I walked into my dressing room to address the bump on my forehead.

Samantha quickly tried to cover the receiver, but it was too late. Lexi had over heard everything.

"A Surprise birthday party?" I chuckled to myself. "That's pretty cool… maybe Harry is not that bad of a guy, after all?"

Alex smiled deviously. "A birthday party? Well this ought to be fun."

Sam screamed into the phone, "Alex don't!"

Lexi snickered and then gloated. "Ha! Ha! I knew it! I'm psychic. See you tonight Sam!" Then Lexi hit the end button on her iPhone.

Astral Charlie bolted out of Lexi's apartment and back to Charlie at the T.V. studio. He entered the station just in time to catch Samantha giving the new production assistant an earful.

Samantha furiously walked up to the PA "Hey! Hey you!"

Steve, the new PA on set, turned around oblivious of his actions. "Hello. How can I help you?"

Sam sneered. "You can help me by keeping your big mouth shut."

"Excuse me?" Steve said, as he stared at Sam in shock.

Samantha cocked her head. "You're not excused. Weren't you at the meeting?"

Steve shook his head no. "What meeting?"

Samantha pushed her blonde locks out of her face. "The meeting where Harry explained that Charlie's birthday party was a surprise!?"

Steve covered his mouth. "Oh no! I'm sorry. I didn't know."

Samantha glared at Steve. "Well don't tell me you're sorry Steve. You better just hope he doesn't mention it to Harry or your ass is grass!"

Steve grabbed his head. "Oh shit! Shit, shit, shit! I can't lose this job."

Samantha took a deep breath. "Okay, well I'll tell you what… if you help me out with something Steve, I'll smooth this whole thing over for you."

Steve looked relieved and happy to oblige. "What is it? I'll do anything."

Sam glared at Steve. "You weren't at the meeting, but if you were you would know that tonight is a pretty important night. Nothing can go wrong. Harry is trying to close a two picture deal, staring Charlie."

"Wow!" Steve exclaimed.

Sam rolled her eyes. "Big freaking whoop. I don't know who'd want to watch that creep on the big screen, but that is beside the point."

Steve pushed on the bridge of his glasses. "Oh I don't know… I think the public is pretty interested in his life."

Sam gritted her teeth. "Cut the crap Steve! Thanks to your little fuck up I now have a crazy woman planning to come to Charlie's Birthday party and ruin it."

"Oh no!" Steve gasped.

Samantha grabbed Steve by the collar, knocking off his glasses. "You have to help me Steve!" Sam gripped Steve's shirt tighter.

"Alright, I'll do it!" Steve moaned

Samantha released her grip from Steve's collar. "Excellent!" She pulled her iPhone out of her purse, searching for a photo of Lexi. "This is a picture of Lexi." Sam showed Steve a newspaper clipping from *Four Golden Stars*."

Steve grabbed Samantha's iPhone. "I saw this movie. It was really touching."

Samantha smirked. "Great Steve. I'm glad to hear that you feel that way."

"Didn't it win an award?" He said.

Samantha took a deep breath. "Yes it did Steve. It won best picture at TIFF and the Cannes Palme D'Or award for best picture, but of course Charlie ignored that bit of information and trashed it regardless of its high acclaim. He made sexist comments, which made Lexi look like a total fool."

Steve shook his head and sighed as he stared at Samantha's cleavage. "It figures."

Sam snapped her fingers in Steve's face trying to draw his attention upwards. "Up here Steve. I'm up here." Steve's face turned bright red as Sam moaned. "Let me spell it out for you Steve. I was on the phone with Lexi trying to make her forget Charlie's awful review when you opened your big fat mouth about where he would be tonight."

"Oh shit! I'm sorry." Steve shrugged his shoulders. "I didn't know!"

Sam shook her head. "It doesn't matter now. What matters is that Lexi is going to show up tonight REALLY PISSED OFF!"

Steve seemed sincerely concerned. "What do you want me to do?"

"That's a very good question Steve. I want you to guard the entrance of La Mystique and under no circumstance are you allowed to let her in."

Steve whined. "But how am I supposed to do that?"

Samantha shrugged her shoulders. "That's your problem Steve! Look…if Harry finds out you were the one who spilled the beans on his little production and that's why a crazy redhead is at his party ready to hunt down his "super star" you're going to have a lot more to worry about than your job. You like your knee caps, right Steve?" Steve's face went blank. Samantha smirked and then without blinking an eye she continued, "Look, it's easy. Just don't screw it up." Then she turned around and walked off the set shaking inside from fear and anger.

Astral Charlie flew after Sam impressed by her take-charge attitude. "Alright! Great work!" He tried to give her a high-five, but of course she ignored him. Astral Charlie put his hand down. "Okay, let me see if I got this plan straight. When we arrive at the party you and that moron over there are going to guard the door and I am going to make sure that we don't do anything stupid." Astral Charlie looked up at the clock on the wall. "It's almost time for the party to begin. You better hurry up!" Samantha walked out of the studio door and Astral Charlie disappeared from the T.V. station.

IT'S A CELEBRATION

Chapter Nine

La Mystique was a mob scene when I showed up; it was filled with paparazzi and fans holding up signs that read, "We Love You Snake" and "Two Thumbs Up For The Angry Movie Guy!" Flashes went off in my face as I tried to make my way through the unruly crowd. From across the room, I could see Harry sitting in between three buxom beauties and I pushed my way through the crowd of guests.

Every person I passed yelled out, "Happy Birthday Charlie!"

The energy in the room was flowing; everybody who was anybody was at the party. The female maître d, a Japanese-American part-time model was as cutthroat with the crowd as a big burly bouncer. She was hyper-vigilant, checking and double-checking the star-studded guest list that seemed to go on for days before letting a soul enter. People were lined up around the corner in anticipation.

Astral Charlie showed up at the party frantic. He flew around the bash searching for me. "Where the hell is he?"

Astral Charlie knew he couldn't play silent Bob any longer or I was going to end up mortified by the woman of my dreams. He saw a crowd of people gathered in one area of the bar and flew over. Crowds of "adoring" fans had momentarily surrounded me and were wishing me a happy birthday. I graciously said my hellos and then continued to make my way over to Harry as fans patted me on the back and wished me happy birthday.

Astral Charlie flew to my side, "Charlie! Something awful is going to happen. The last review you gave was not for a man named Alex; it was for a woman named Alexis!"

I continued to make my way towards Harry as Astral Charlie flew after me. "Where are you going Charlie?! You're not listening to me. The person you gave an awful review to last week was the woman of your dreams! And she's headed here to ruin your party! Maybe even your life Charlie... I'm sorry! I tried to stop her." Astral Charlie watched me walk away and figured it was useless. He couldn't get through to me with all these people around so he decided to look for Sam instead.

I was almost at Harry's table when I spotted Sean, Harry's regular flamboyant waiter. I tried to get his attention, but he was too busy. I felt like he was ignoring me on purpose. Nonetheless, I admired how he dressed up for the occasion; He was wearing skinny black jeans and a stiff white button up dress shirt. If it weren't for the fact that he was running around frazzled, taking drink orders I would have assumed that he was one of the guests. Sean pushed his way through the crowd, dodging one socialite after the next until a heavyset woman from the station bumped into him blocking his way. The woman was carrying an enormous present, which I assumed was for me.

"I brought Charlie a present." She squealed in a high-pitched annoying voice as she looked towards me for recognition.

Sean glared at the woman's backside as she continued to block his way. "And it's the biggest one in the house. I know because I checked the table of gifts." The woman smiled, showing off the tiny gap between her two front teeth. "Where do you want me to put it Charlie?"

Harry noticed the woman crowding me with her oversized gift and rushed to my side.

"I can't let the man of the hour stand. Let me take care of this for you Charlie."

Harry walked up to the plump woman.

"Hi. What's your name?"

The woman smiled and cheerfully replied. "Lydia."

Harry grinned at Lydia. "Lydia, why don't you do me a favor and set the gift on the table in the back?"

Lydia nodded her head. "Sure thing, Harry. You won't forget me at Christmas time, will you?"

Harry chuckled. "Of course not Lena…"

The woman abruptly stopped and turned around. "It's Lydia."

Harry nodded his head. "Right, that's what I said."

The woman peered over the top of the gift at Harry. "Go ahead, set it down right over there." Harry pointed to a table in the back of the restaurant where a four piece jazz band was setting up on a small makeshift stage.

Lydia looked around her. "You sure there's nowhere closer? It's kind of heavy."

Harry shook his head. "Nope. Not a chance. We got to have these tables empty Lena for our Hollywood big shots. You understand, right?" She nodded her head and waddled off as Harry and I settled in.

I watched as the room filled up making it more and more uncomfortable for the staff to do their jobs. Astral Charlie witnessed Sean shriek as his favorite black suede shoes got ruined by one of my hoity-toity guests. Sean glared at the platinum blonde's backside as she sauntered off.

"That better have been Paris Hilton, otherwise…" Another guest spilled their drink on Sean before he could complete his sentence. "Oh my God! One day I'll be more famous than all of you!" Sean muttered to himself as he stomped off, holding an empty glass.

Harry slid up next to me and slapped me on the back. "So what do you think? Killer party right?"

I nodded my head and blushed, embarrassed by how needy I was feeling. Harry smiled and wrapped his arm around me. "Only the best for my boy!" Harry grabbed my knee beneath the table and shouted as he puffed on an expensive cigar. "Tell me your enjoying yourself Charlie!"

"It's great!" I said. "I almost forgot how I pissed half of my goddamn life away!" I sipped a Black label scotch on the rocks and watched as the crowd chatted with one another. I joked with Harry like I didn't have a care in the world. Hours passed and I was hammered. All of a sudden, the crowd got quiet and Sean walked out from the kitchen with a gigantic chocolate cake in the shape of a middle finger, covered with sparklers. The cake was inscribed: *We love you Angry Movie Guy!*

Sean flamboyantly sang, leading the crowd in song. "Happy birthday to you, happy birthday to you! Happy Birthday, dear Charlie… Happy Birthday to you!"

The guest cheered in unison as I blew out the candles.

Harry hugged me. "Happy Birthday Charlie!"

I blushed as they fussed over me, even though I knew it was probably because Harry had promised the staff an extra Christmas bonus.

Meanwhile, Samantha, Steve and Astral Charlie all guarded the door like a hawk. Sam knew how cunning Lexi was when she wanted something and neither the Japanese Princess at the door, or Steve the paranoid PA, would be able to stop Lexi if she wanted in bad enough. Sam peered at the guests still waiting in line and elbowed Steve.

"You have to look carefully, because if I know Lexi she didn't come dressed like the other guests. She'll be in some sort of disguise." Sam looked down at her phone that was buzzing. "I've got to get this. Watch the door Steve!" Steve nodded his head as Sam answered the phone. "Hello?"

Gary blurted out. "Any sign of Lexi?"

Sam stepped to the side shouting into her phone. "Not yet, but I doubt she's going to let this slide Gary."

Astral Charlie tried to listen in, but it was too noisy to hear anything.

Gary yelled, "She promised me she wouldn't do anything Sam. I think you can put your mind at ease."

Sam scoffed. "No offense Gary, but you obviously don't know Alex. One day, when I was eight years old my dad forgot to pick me up after school because he was drunk. Lexi was so upset she decided to teach him a lesson. She crushed up flies for the next six months and stuck them in his bourbon until he finally caught her. My father gave Lexi a beating that would make a grown man cry, but that didn't stop Lexi from giving him a piece of her mind. So if you think your little pep talk convinced her to just throw in the towel, you're sadly mistaken. Now I've got to go Gary before Lexi slips by me."

Sam hung up the phone and went back to examining the guests in line. Unbeknownst to Samantha, Lexi had already managed to slip by in a disguise, just as Sam suspected.

Lexi walked in while Sam was on the phone wearing a long black wig and carrying a huge camera case. She flashed a badge at the Japanese model and told her she was working for Hampton's magazine. The door model stared at Lexi's badge for an uncomfortable amount of time. Lexi was afraid she would be accused of being an imposter, but then a small fight broke out at the bar distracting the Japanese Princess. Lexi snapped a picture and tried to show the up-tight female bouncer, but she was uninterested. She waived Lexi into the party and told the rest of the guest to wait in line until she returned.

Lexi scooted around the room in disguise taking pictures of the guests till she found an un-locked private restroom on the second floor. She then bribed a staff member to stash the clothes she was wearing in the back of the kitchen. The barely English-speaking employee gladly accepted Lexi's generous payoff and told her that her belongings would be safe with him. Minutes later, Lexi emerged from the bathroom in an expensive evening gown she had stuffed in her case.

Astral Charlie was the first to discover Lexi. He yelped at the sight of her. Lexi looked stunning. She was dressed like she was attending a Hollywood red carpet event, but he knew she was prepared to rip Charlie a new one. He flew up to her and pleaded with her.

"Please don't do this. I'm an idiot. I can't help myself. I have low self-esteem."

Lexi ignored Astral Charlie and continued to strut over to an Italian designer she knew who drapes for Givenchy and said hello. The tall, dark and handsome designer gushed at the sight of Lexi in her gown. All the guests turned as he boisterously admired her dress. Sam overheard the ruckus and noticed Lexi being fawned over. She bolted to her side with Steve in tow and pleaded with her.

"Alex! Don't do this!"

Samantha pinched the small of Lexi's arm, but Lexi didn't budge.

She whispered, "Don't even try to stop me Sam. This is between me and that demon in disguise."

I was still oblivious to the news that my dream girl had arrived at the party. I cut a few slices of cake for my guests. "I am actually having a great time Harry and the guests seem to be having fun too. Right?" I looked toward Harry for reassurance.

"It's a party Charlie!" Harry climbed up on top of the table and yelled to the bartender. "Shots all around!" The bartender gave Harry a "thumbs up" and began pouring.

Alex sauntered across the room while Sam and Steve tried to stop her without causing a scene. Harry looked over and spotted Lexi and blushed with excitement. "Wow! Now she's a show stopper!"

I looked up at Harry drooling over the site of a woman. "What are you talking about Harry? Who is?" Harry ignored me and whistled at Alex, so I climbed up on the booth to see what all the fuss was about. My heart skipped a beat and I nearly fell off the table at the site of her. "It's her Harry. She's here! It's a miracle!" I watched in disbelief as the crowd swallowed her up.

Astral Charlie and Samantha we're becoming more agitated and looked to Steve for help. "Do something Steve!"

Steve did the only thing he could think of… he ran to get help.

Sam pleaded with Lexi. "I don't know how you did it Lexi, but you better just turn around and leave before it's too late."

Lexi blurted out, "Not before I give that troll a piece of my mind!"

Steve returned with the Japanese Princess. "What seems to be the problem?" She sneered.

Alex turned towards the model who now noticed she had been duped. "I knew that press badge was a fake. Okay that's it. The gig is up. It's time to pack it up sweety!"

Sam glared at Lexi. "So that's how you did it. You posed as the paparazzi."

Steve smiled and elbowed Sam. "Oh, she's good."

Lexi began to scream as Steve and the door Princess tried to grab her arm. "Get your hands off of me! I just want to speak with him!" Alex cocked her head and turned towards Steve. "You know that saying, don't you Steve? I may not know karate, but I know crazy." Steve abruptly dropped Lexi's arm and backed away, dumbfounded by Lexi's remark.

At this point the crowd cleared and I realized my dream girl was in trouble. I jumped off the table and pushed my way through the crowd. Harry followed in hot pursuit. As I approached her I realized my assistant was escorting her towards the door.

"Take your hands off of her!" I screamed.

Alex glared at me, puzzled by my sincerity. I smiled at my dream girl. "Hi! How did you know about the party? I mean, don't get me wrong, I'm ecstatic that you're here. But how…?"

Samantha gave Steve a kick in the rear end and he spoke up. "I'm sorry Charlie, she isn't on the guest list. I tried to stop her at the door, but she just barged through."

I turned towards Steve. "And you are?"

The young PA was sweating bullets. "I'm the new PA on the show, names Steve." Steve sheepishly stuck out his hand. I nodded my head. "Right… right, I remember you. You can take your hands off of her Steve." Steve looked at Sam, waiting for her approval.

Harry took his hat off, scratching his head. "What's the big deal? Charlie knows her and he's happy to see her. Harry turned and looked at my face all lit up. "Look at the man, I've never seen him more excited!"

Alex laughed and put her hands on her hips. "Yeah, I think that's funny! You're ecstatic to see me after you tried to ruin my career?!"

"Huh," I said bewildered. I saw Sean come out of the kitchen and I waived him over. "Sean, come here! Can you bring this stunning woman a drink?"

Astral Charlie began to whimper. "Oh, Charlie you don't understand. She hates you!"

Alex looked at me with disgust in her eyes. "Can you get me a drink? Oh no! No, the 'Snake' isn't going to charm me. That's not how this is going down. No way. No how!"

I looked at my dream girl perplexed. "Okay... then can you at least tell me how I ruined your career?"

Lexi's eyes nearly popped out of her head. "HOW? Does *Four Golden Stars* ring a bell?"

I shrugged my shoulders. "Yes... but what in the world does that have to do with you?"

Alex backed away from Charlie. "What does it have to do with me? You really have no idea who I am, do you?"

I smiled shyly at her. "Well I'm afraid I left before we were ever formally introduced."

Alex took a deep breath. "I am Alex Rasner. The writer and the director of the worst thing you've seen since *Steel Doves,* which I might add was a movie I loved. And if I recall, you called me a special person with a camera. The winner of the Special Olympics Charity event!"

Astral Charlie covered his eyes. "I can't watch!"

I now realized what I had done and I turned to Harry for help, but of course Harry did nothing. I felt more pathetic than I had in years. I turned back towards Alex. "You're him? You're Alex? "

Just then, Sean returned with a drink for Alex. "Ooohhh! It looks like we're having a lover's quarrel?!"

I glared at Sean. "Stay out of this! There isn't going to be a fight!"

Sean put his hands on his hips, "There isn't?"

I was sweating from the embarrassing scene. I yelled, "No!"

Sean smirked and said, "Well then, will you please hand the lady this Cosmo?"

I picked the Cosmo up off the tray and handed it to Alex who immediately threw it back into my face. I watched in disbelief as people snapped numerous pictures on their camera phones.

Sean put his hand back on his hips. "Now, where I come from those are fighting words!"

Harry yelled out, "Arrest her!"

Sam stepped back humiliated; She tried to grab Lexi by the arm. "Lexi! Let's go, before you get yourself into trouble!"

Harry took off his hat, revealing his glistening baldhead. "She's already in trouble!"

I turned to Harry. "Just calm down! I'm the one who got a drink thrown in my face and if I say I'm okay then everything is okay." I wiped my face with a napkin that Sean handed to me and turned back to Alex. "There isn't going to be any fight is there? I think you made your point..." Before I could complete the thought Alex hauled off and belted me in the face as Sean began to shout. "Fight! Fight! Fight!" At that moment, everything went black and I hit the floor.

Astral Charlie hovered over me concerned for my well-being. "Wake up Charlie!" Minutes later, I opened my eyes and found a group of people huddled around me, fanning me with a menu.

I mumbled, "Crackers, that's just crackers!"

Sean yelled to the crowd. "He's alive!"

Through blurred vision, I tried to interpret what I was seeing. The woman I'd fallen in love with was standing motionless as the paparazzi snapped numerous photographs of her. The crowd was in a frenzy posting pictures on every social feed they could think of.

I heard Sean tell a guest, "You know I can't quite put my finger on it, but there is something about that girl that I simply adore. She's fierce!"

Harry turned to Sean. "Not another word out of you." Harry then turned his attention to Alex, "And as for you, you little hellion... just stay clear of him, you hear me? If you have anything to say you can tell it to our lawyers."

I tried to get up. "Harry, don't worry. It's okay, really."

Harry leaned in close to my face whispering, "It's better than okay. You can't buy this kind of publicity and believe me I've tried." I sat up holding my head and noticed the two movie executives Harry had invited standing on their chairs proudly chatting to one another.

I then watched two police officers make their way through the crowd. Alex also noticed them coming towards her with handcuffs drawn and she pushed her way back to my side.

Sam tried to grab her. "Just stop before it's too late Lexi!"

Harry put his arms out to protect me, but I stopped him. "It's okay," I foolishly said, "I want to hear what she has to say."

Alex leaned in close. "The police are here and they are going to want to take me away."

I tried to get up. "Don't worry, they don't have to."

Alex looked behind her and saw the two burly cops inching towards her. "No, they will. But there's something I want you to know before that happens."

I looked at her with doe eyes, pushing Harry's hands out of the way. "What is it?"

Alex's face was bright red with anger as she spoke through gritted teeth. "I want you to know… that no matter what happens I hate you more than anyone in the entire universe!" Then Lexi slapped me across the face so hard that she left her handprint on my cheek. Harry softened the blow by catching my head as I passed out again. I later heard that the cops broke through the crowd and grabbed Alex by the arms.

They shouted, "Freeze! You're under arrest!"

Then a crowd of people followed Lexi outside the restaurant as the police led her towards a police car parked right out front of La

Mystique. Samantha, Steve, Astral Charlie and Sean the waiter hurried after Lexi as the cops read her rights to her.

"You have the right to remain silent, anything you say can and will be used against you...."

Sean called out after her, "Baby, do not tell them anything until you have a lawyer! Remember the Fifth Amendment! You're my Joan of Arc!"

I'M A BELIEVER

Chapter Ten

I woke up the following morning in a dreary hospital bed with a small bandage on the bridge of my nose and both eyes bruised. My mind was playing tricks on me. For a second, I thought maybe I died and this was the waiting room for Hell. No such luck!

A nurse walked in, reminiscent of my deceased mother. "Mom?" I said, "What are you doing here?"

The bubbly nurse smiled and checked my bandage. "It's all right. You just need your rest Charlie. Everything is going to be okay."

"No, it's not!" I exclaimed, as I grabbed the nurse by the arm and poured my heart out. "I ruined everything. I ruined someone's dream. In fact, I ruined a lot of people's dreams. Mine included."

The nurse gently removed my hand from her arm. "That sounds rather harsh Mr. Zimmerman."

Shaking my head solemnly I reiterated, "I'm afraid it's the truth."

The nurse walked around my bed and added a clear fluid to one of the tubes sticking out of my nose. I winced in pain as she put her hand on my head to check my bumps and bruises.

"Well anytime I've made a mess in my life Charlie, I just look for a way to clean it up."

I smiled and said, "You know what? You're right. I just have to clean it up. Thanks Mom."

The nurse shook her head as I passed out. A few hours later I woke up screaming. "Mom!"

Harry had been waiting for me to wake up and scrambled to my bedside.

"Charlie! You're awake. You really must have hit your head, buddy." He waived his hands in front of my face. "It's just me, your old pal, Harry."

I looked at Harry confused and groggy from the sedative the nurse had given me. Harry pulled a chair up beside the bed.

"How are you feeling?"

I squinted in pain from the sight of Harry's brightly colored flowered shirt. "Like I've been making love to a bag of broken glass."

Harry shook his head. "Yeah I bet. For a minute there, I thought I was going to have to find a replacement for you on the show." Harry let out a loud laugh. "I'm just kidding! How's the head?"

"Throbbing," I murmured.

Harry took his hat off and wiped some sweat from his brow. "Well, you don't have to worry about that little hussy any longer. I made sure she's where she belongs, in jail."

I bolted to attention. "What do you mean she's in jail?"

Harry stood up and looked at himself in the mirror. "What did you expect? She knocked you unconscious." I cringed at his words, but it didn't stop Harry from continuing to rub it in my face. "That sweet piece of ass almost killed you. She's deranged and a complete menace to society."

I struggled with the tubes, trying to remove them. "I deserved it Harry! I've got to get her out of there!"

Harry looked baffled. "I don't think that's a good idea, Charlie."

I slid out of bed, yanking the tubes out of my nose as I put on my pants, exposing myself to Harry in the process. Harry blocked his eyes.

"Whoa! What are you doing buddy?"

I struggled with my pants. "I've got to get out of here!" Harry rang the bell, alerting the nurse.

"Have you lost your mind Charlie?" He began to call down the hallway. "Nurse! Nurse!"

The bubbly nurse ran into the room. "What is it?"

Harry pointed at me. "He's trying to escape. Now, is that really smart? He could have a concussion or God knows what else? Tell him!"

I grabbed the nurse and intensely stared into her eyes. "The woman of my dreams is in jail because of me and if I don't get to her she's liable to be released back into the world and I'll never see her again." I ran out of the hospital room and down the hallway.

Harry screamed, "Charlie stop!" Then Harry grabbed the nurse and demanded she put an end to my erratic behavior. "Nurse do something, he's completely lost it!"

The nurse looked at Harry and calmly removed his hand. "Actually he doesn't have a concussion or a broken nose or anything. We kept him overnight for observation, but he's totally fine."

Harry grabbed his hat. "You've got to be kidding me?" He watched as I raced back down the hospital hallway like a maniac.

Harry snorted. "He's fine?"

The nurse looked at me concerned. "Yes?"

"See, I'm fine!" I gloated as I ran back into the hospital room, wild-eyed like a crazy person to grab my evening jacket.

With pleasant modesty the nurse grabbed me as I attempted to exit the room. "He's free to go... once we discharge him."

Harry scoffed. "You're telling me he's fine? Look at him." I looked like an utter disaster with bandages on my face and my robe tucked into my pants. "He's on-air talent. He can't be seen like this." Harry grunted as I put on my shoes.

"Look on the bright side Harry... with this face I'll appeal to the raccoon demographic you have always wanted to tap into." I grinned at Harry revealing a tooth still covered with blood.

"Ugh! That's awful!" Harry averted his eyes.

I put my arm around the nurse's shoulder. "I have a question for you. Would you be so kind as to show me where I may get discharged?"

The nurse smiled and giggled. "Sure, you can follow me Mr. Zimmerman. But you might want to take off your robe. I don't think they will discharge you like that."

I pulled off my robe and patted my oversized paunch with a boyish charm. "Is this more of what you had in mind?"

The nurse was amused. "Not exactly. I thought you might want to put on a shirt or something." Yanking my shirt out of the closet I examined it. It was covered in bloodstains.

I innocently looked at the nurse. "I'm about to break the woman I love out of jail. I don't think I should show up with stains on my shirt. Do you?"

The nurse picked up my medical chart and began the discharge process. "Well that depends on your options."

I squinted my eyes. "Meaning?"

She whispered, "Meaning, if the robe is your only other option, I would go with the blood stained shirt."

I nodded my head in agreement. "I see your point. Maybe I'll stop off and pick something up on the way over."

The nurse smiled and walked out of the room. "I think that would be a good idea. Now let's get you out of here so you can go break the little lady out of jail." I filled out the paperwork and convinced Harry to drive me over to the police station.

Astral Charlie flew into the entrance of the hospital, wearing a smock. He was just in time to see Harry and I leave.

"Where are you going?" Astral Charlie flew up to the nurse who had been taking care of me. "Your letting him get away?!" He then flew up to the sliding door disappointed. "I was just about to perform surgery on that gunshot wound that came in!" Astral Charlie dropped his surgical tools, tossed off his white coat and flew full speed ahead out of the hospital and into Harry's BMW. He was surprised to see Charlie who was sitting in the front seat like a chump. "They let you leave like that? Who is running that hospital, chimpanzees?"

Harry slammed the trunk of his BMW and then got into the driver's seat. He handed me a blue polo crew neck shirt. "Here, put this on. You look hideous." Harry continued to voice his frustrations as he pulled out of the hospital parking lot. "I can't believe I'm driving you to break the woman out of jail who put you in the hospital."

I shook my head. "Me either, actually."

Harry looked irritated. "This must be the stupidest thing I've ever done."

I pulled down the vanity mirror and examined my face. "I have to agree with you, she really did a number on me."

Harry rubbed his baldhead. "Yeah! You're just figuring that out now?"

I rolled down the window to get some fresh air. I was feeling faint, but I didn't want Harry to know. "Is it hot in here or is it just me?"

Harry cringed at my fuzzy body. "Well, with that bear you're wearing I can see why you might be a little warm. Would you pull down that shirt for God's sakes, you're scaring me. I can see you never did use that gym membership I gave you."

I wasn't in the mood for his insults. "Cut the crap Harry." I yanked on the shirt, but it was at least two sizes too small.

Harry began to laugh. "You look like a beach whale on a holiday away from your natural habitat."

I looked down at myself. My gut was sticking out of the bottom of the shirt. I tried to pull it down again, but I ripped the sleeves. "What do you think?"

Harry pulled up to a stoplight. "I think if you're trying to get her back for what she did to you that this should do the trick." "Very funny Harry."

We pulled up to a streetlight, just a block away from the precinct and to my surprise the same little girl with the brunette pigtails was seated in the back seat of her mother's SUV. I looked out my window and glared at the little brat. Harry honked his horn and waived to her. The toothless little brat smiled and then mouthed the words, "Buzz off!" I flipped her the bird as Harry pulled away.

Seconds later, we pulled into the mid-town police booking station. Harry parked his BMW in the back of the lot and tried to persuade me to change my mind.

"You're not really going to do this, are you?"

I snarled. "Yes Harry. Now are you going to pull up or do I have to get out and walk the rest of the way?" I opened the car door to reiterate my point.

Harry looked at my bruised face and then reluctantly agreed. "I'll pull up."

I entered the police station, like a bat out of hell. I ran up to the desk and began tapping on a silver bell. "I'm here to see Alex." I turned around looking for Harry's help, but he was taking his sweet time parking the car.

Astral Charlie slammed his hands on the counter. "Give us the girl or I'll be forced to perform a vasectomy without pain killers!" Astral Charlie grabbed a pair of scissors off the desk and held them up. The overweight male rookie officer looked at my face as he shoved a glazed doughnut into his mouth.

"I think you're talking about Alex Rasner. We took her in last night after she punched some poor fellow."

I smiled and put my hand over my heart. "Yes, that's her."

The police officer laughed. "So you're the guy she beat up?"

I put my hand up to correct the officer. "Punched officer."

The sergeant was getting a kick out of the situation. He turned his chair to face his co-workers. "Yo Rickie, this is the chump I was telling you about." The guys in the back started to get up from their chairs chuckling at the sight of my bruised face. "Oh man, she really did a number on you!" They all started to snicker.

Harry walked in catching the end of their conversation and chimed in. "Beat up and put in jail as a pre-caution, yes sergeant."

A loud-mouthed officer sitting in the back stood up. "What was it, a domestic dispute or something?"

I smiled, "I hope that one day that will be the case."

The desk agent shook his head. "The bail is set at…"

I took out my wallet. "I've got it, whatever it is. Just please get her out of there."

I turned to Harry. "You deal with that." I put my wallet away. The sergeant looked at Harry and then at me.

"You sure you know what you're doing buddy? She messed you up pretty bad!"

I read the name on the officers' badge. "I appreciate your concern Officer Higgins, but I know what I'm doing." The officer set the release paperwork down on the counter.

"Alright, but for your own protection I'm going to have to ask you to wait outside while I tell her the news of who is paying for her release."

I cut him off. "Is that really necessary?"

He looked at my ridiculous get up and said, "Yes, I believe it is Sir."

Harry walked up to me. "Charlie, why don't you grab some fresh air like the officer said and I'll deal with the paperwork, alright?"

I limped to the door. "Fine!" I said, as I exited the precinct and sat on the steps outside." I saw the rookie give Harry a look of warning as I walked out the door.

Astral Charlie decided to stay behind to snoop. He overheard Harry trying to pry information out of the rookie. "How is she officer?"

The young officer tipped his hat. "I'd say she's doing okay under the circumstance. Although, she did have the ladies pretty worked up last night."

Harry seemed concerned. "What do you mean?"

The officer took his hat off and rubbed his forehead. "She told them how she landed the night in the slammer and they ate it up. They were in there enthusiastically hooting and hollering."

Harry took off his hat and rubbed his head mimicking the officer. "Really?"

The officer shook his head. "Yup, and these are not the type of ladies who hoot and holler."

Astral Charlie piped up, "Ooh wee! I'm just going to fly back there and check out the jail cell."

Harry wiped the sweat off his head. "On second thought, maybe we should just leave her in there."

The officer shook his head and pointed to the cashier. "No can do. You already signed the release. You got to pay the piper and hope for the best." Harry groaned as he watched the sergeant walk off.

Astral Charlie entered the jail cell. He thought he would try and butter up Alex before she walked out of the precinct and came into contact with me pathetically sitting on the front steps of the precinct battered and bruised. Astral Charlie knew I had every intention of chasing Alex to the ends of the earth even if it meant that I ruined my *Angry Movie Guy* reputation by coming across like a battered woman in a horrible sensational American after school TV drama. Astral Charlie flew up to Alex and began whispering sweet nothings into her ear as she slept on the metal bench in her glamorous gown.

"You are more than just my Valentine…you are my everything. Astral Charlie began to sing, *My Little Valentine*, by Frank Sinatra."

The guard walked up to Alex's jail cell and began tapping his patrol stick on the cell to wake Alex up. "Alex Rasner you just made bail. You are free to go."

Alex stood up confused. "How? I mean… that's it?"

The guard looked annoyed. "All I know is two guys came here and one of them with a busted face paid bail."

Alex fidgeted nervously. "Could you be more specific please?"

"Look lady. I don't know and I don't care. But, if you want to get out of here, I suggest you get moving."

Alex turned towards the other woman in the cell.

A big black woman stood up and spoke in a low-pitched voice. "Good luck Alex. We will all be rooting for you, won't we?"

The other woman in the jail cell hollered. "That's right! If that joker tries to play you for a fool…Big Mama is gonna show em' whose boss!" Big Mamma started pounding her fist into her hand. Astral Charlie watched Big Mamma pound her fist and swallowed hard.

Then a little scrawny hooker jumped up on the steel bed and yelled at the top of her lungs. "Don't let him give you no shit! Remember that chokehold I showed you Alex!"

Big Mamma grabbed the scrawny hooker and demonstrated it for her one more time. Alex looked down at the hooker in the chokehold and smiled. "I'll remember."

Another woman yelled out flashing her gold teeth. "But don't forget to take his money first and then whoop his ass!"

Alex gave Big Mamma a hug. "That's great advice! Thanks everybody!"

Astral Charlie flew up to Alex's side. "Your not really going to try and put me in a chokehold… are you?"

The guard impatiently knocked his patrol stick on the jail cell again. "Alright ladies, break it up. This isn't a going away party. Move it along." Alex waived goodbye to the other women and walked out of the cell. She gathered her belongings and made a short phone call to Sam for a ride home. The rookie observed Alex pensively as she signed the release paperwork. He was about to inform her that I was outside waiting for her, but she bolted out of the station before he had the chance.

Astral Charlie flew out behind her yelling, "The service here sucks! We're never coming back!"

I had anxiously been eyeing the police headquarters waiting for Lexi to exit the precinct. The minute she walked out the door I yelled at Harry.

"Let's go. She's getting away."

We eagerly ran after Alex as she tried to walk faster. I yelled, "Alex! Alex, wait!" Alex broke out into a full sprint.

Harry stopped, out of breath. "Go ahead, I'll catch up."

Astral Charlie valiantly flew ahead and stuck his hand out in front of Alex motioning for her to stop. "Stop in the name of love!"

I finally caught up to Alex as she reached the curb. There was nowhere else to run. I coolly approached her and said, "Hey there!" She ignored me, turning her back on me.

Harry walked up beside me and bent over, panting like an overweight chain smoker. "Hello, Miss." I nudged him to cool it. Harry gave me an annoyed look. "What?" He stood up and put his hand on his side. "She doesn't want to speak with you Charlie. You're wasting your time."

To counter act Harry's negative comment I overcompensated with bold confidence. "Why don't you run along Harry and let us talk."

Harry looked at me like I'd gone mad. I handed him five dollars. "Here…pick me up a coffee from Starbucks. I'm just going to wait here and make sure she gets home okay."

Harry took his cowboy hat off and wiped the sweat off his brow. "You want me to leave you alone with her?"

I kicked him and stammered. "Yes. Don't worry Harry, I'll be fine."

Astral Charlie hovered over me. "Don't worry Harry, I'll protect him."

Harry sighed. "Fine. Do you have the pepper spray I gave you just in case she acts up again?" Alex turned around and stared at us like we were two of the biggest idiots she'd ever met.

I nudged him. "Go Harry!"

Harry shook his head and walked off checking out Alex's butt like a creep. "That is one fine piece of ass."

Alex glared at me. "I hope you don't expect me to thank you for springing me?"

I smiled like a church kid on Sunday who wanted to be forgiven for his sins. "Ah no, I'd actually like to forget this ever happened. Maybe we could start over like how it was when we first met at the showing of *Lost in Her Eyes*."

She turned her back to me. "Just forget it, Charlie."

"Are you sure you won't reconsider?" I said, sheepishly.

Alex glared at me. "Not a chance."

"Well can I at least give you a lift?"

Alex walked away. I stared at the sun shining on her back. "I have a friend on the way," she said as I coyly scooted up to her side.

"Okay. Well, I guess I'll just wait here till they arrive. Don't mind me." I casually spoke to her as if we were having a cup of coffee at a little café. "I'm feeling a little better." Alex took a few steps away from me, so I began to exaggerate the story with the hope of receiving her sympathy. "The doctors said it was only a minor concussion. They say the hair should grow back. I kind of have a gouge in the back here." I turned to show her. "See? Ten stitches. The doctor said I was real lucky. It's kind of amazing, I mean I always knew I had a glass jaw but... so do you work out?"

Alex whipped her head around; tears filled her eyes as she strongly advised me to leave. "You should go Charlie. Your friend is waiting for you."

I looked back at Harry who had pulled into the front of the station in his BMW. "Harry? He can wait. Besides, I'm enjoying talking with you."

Astral Charlie looked worried. He started to pull on my shirt. "We should go Charlie!" Harry jumped out of his BMW with his radio blasting the song, *This Is How We Do,* by Katy Perry.

171

Harry screamed, "She's going to blow Charlie! Watch out!"

Alex's chest was heaving from anger. "I really think you should go before I end up back in jail."

Harry had his arm out ready to yank me from her side until I fell to my knees like a complete moron. "It's just that I think I'm in love with you."

Alex's eyes nearly popped out of her head as I stared up at her on bended knees, like a complete idiot with my gut hanging out of Harry's polo shirt.

Alex looked wild. "What! Are you mad?"

I guarded myself, placing my hands over my head ripping Harry's shirt even further. "I know it sounds crazy, but it's true."

Seconds later, Samantha drove up in her Austin Mini Coop and parked it right next to Harry's BMW. She turned off the tail end of the song, *Sounds of the Universe* and calmly exited her vehicle. She was attempting to protect her identity by wearing an OBEY cap and sunglasses.

She scooted up to Lexi's side and whispered, "Alex… the cops are gathering outside the station. I say we go before you spend another night in jail."

Alex had her arm raised ready to punch me again until she noticed Samantha standing beside her. A look of relief swept across Alex's face and then quickly dissipated as I blurted out, "I know you from somewhere?"

Astral Charlie was attempting to block the cops view. "Go back inside. Nothing to see here."

Harry grabbed me by the arm. "What in God's name are you doing Charlie? Get up! She wants to kill you."

Sam tugged on Alex's wrinkled red gown, whispering, "Let's get out of here Alex."

Alex hugged Sam. "Okay."

Sam quickly ushered Alex towards her mini coop while Harry helped me off the ground. I squinted my eyes trying to place the woman in hiding.

I snapped my fingers and said, "I got it! You work on my show!"

Samantha pulled down her cap, trying to cover her face. "No, no I don't."

I rushed to her side and peered into her shaded Ralph Lauren sunglasses. "Drop the act!"

Sam huffed. "Okay. Fine. I do!"

Alex ran back over to where I was standing and stood in front of Sam protecting her. "One thing has nothing to do with the other, so if you as much as think of firing my cousin I'll have my lawyer on your ass..."

I cut Alex off by grabbing Samantha's hand and shaking it. "Your cousin? That's great! It's Samantha, right?"

Samantha looked at Alex confused. "Uh, yeah."

I smiled. "Great! That is just great!" My hands flung up in the air as I did a little dance shaking my paunch as I wiggled. "Make sure you get her home safely. I mean it now. Don't let anything happen to her!"

Harry grabbed me and practically forced me into his BMW. "You've gone nuts! You really, truly have! You know that?" I looked at him perplexed, unaware of how peculiar I was acting as I shimmied into the front seat of his BMW.

"What?" I said, as I basked in my sudden change of luck. Astral Charlie flew into the back seat of Harry's BMW and peered out the back window at the cops.

"Wow! That was a close call Charlie." He leaned over the front seat towards Harry. "If I were you, I'd step on the gas before those coppers decide to come and arrest both of you." Harry glanced out his rearview mirror and deliberately stepped on the gas.

ON & ON

Chapter Eleven

Harry gave me an ear full on the way home. He rattled on and on, but nothing Harry said had any affect on the way I felt about Alex. I was on cloud nine until I walked into my condo and noted a very discerning and distinct smell. There's nothing quite like the smell of fresh cat piss. I opened up all the windows in the house and checked my calendar on the refrigerator. My house cleaner was supposed to have cleaned while I was in the hospital, but the place was a disaster. I pressed play on the answering machine and listened to my maid Sweetie, a Scandinavian Asian woman with a very thick accent.

"Mr. Evans, this is your maid Sweetie. I watch news, but don't know what to do. I came to clean, but lady from animal shelter show up and say I must take cats till Auntie have more room at shelter. She say you won't mind. Just for a few days she say, so I put cats in study. Pussy mean though, don't let me clean... kept hissing at me, so I go."

I deleted the message. "Great! That's all I need, another cat."

Another message played. "Hello Charlie. This is Laura from the animal shelter. I dropped a few more cats to your home yesterday. Unfortunately, your housekeeper seemed a little confused."

I deleted the message and started filling a long line of bowls with cat food. The messages continued to play.

"Charlie? Charlie, are you there? This is your father. Call me back. I saw the news. Are you all right? Let's meet, I have something important I need to discuss with you." I stood up to delete the message and bumped my head on the cupboard.

"Asshole!"

I reluctantly walked into study to check on the cats. It seemed the animal shelter didn't have enough room for another four angry cats and that my condo was the best place to put them. Entering the study, I prepared myself for the worst. "Crackers! That's just crackers!" My new designer curtains were ripped to shreds; they'd pissed on the rug, the pillows and my favorite pair of brown patent leather shoes. "That's it!" I screamed, as I turned around and walked upstairs and fell asleep to the sound of purring cats.

The following day Samantha didn't show up at work. I felt betrayed. Hoping to butter her up, I had made a special visit to Starbucks to order her an iced macchiato, and she hadn't bothered to show up for work. "Why do I even bother?" I muttered to myself, as I watched the employees at the studio scurry by my open dressing room door.

One of the newer crewmembers, a young brunette passed by and peeked in. She noticed I looked upset. "Everything okay, Charlie?"

I sighed. "I'm fine."

"Okay." She said, and then turned to leave.

I called after her, "It's just that my assistant didn't come in today and I really need her help. You don't happen to have her number, do you?"

The bright-eyed, bushy tailed employee delightfully smiled. I could tell she was fresh out of college and eager to please her new boss. She pulled her Galaxy phone out of her back pocket. "Sure Charlie."

I quickly jotted down Samantha's number and then ushered her out of my dressing room.

Samantha was at home lounging. She had just put on a facemask and was about to begin painting her toenails when she glanced down at her beeping iPhone. "Crap!" She set the blue bottle of nail polish on the table and answered my phone call. "Hello?"

"Hello, Samantha? I covered the phone like I was being watched even though I was alone in my dressing room.

Sam began to cough. "Yes, who is this?"

"It's Charlie."

Samantha's voice quivered. "Charlie who?"

I rolled my eyes. "This is your boss Samantha."

Sam sounded alarmed. "Charlie? Is everything okay?"

I moved to the couch in my dressing room. "Everything is fine Samantha. Am I bothering you? They told me you called in sick today."

Samantha coughed louder. "Yeah, I'm pretty sick."

I imagined Samantha's face flushed from the thought of being caught in her pathetic lie. Pulling the phone away from my ear I yelled, "Faker!"

Samantha screamed. "What? No! I'm really sick." She began to cough again.

I yelled. "Faker! Faker!"

Samantha sounded more agitated by the second. "I'm not faking." She tried to exaggerate her cough.

"I'm not buying it, Samantha."

Samantha stopped coughing. "Look Charlie, Alex is my cousin. I want to keep my job but...."

I interrupted her. "Who said anything about your job?"

Samantha sounded shocked. "Oh! Well, I think it's best if we keep as far away from each other as possible."

My voice cracked. "That's crazy. You're my assistant on the show."

Samantha took a deep breath. "Well, I prefer if you didn't call me at home. I mean it's nothing personal against you... it's just kind of weird, you know?"

I went to the dressing room mirror and looked at my bruised face. "I know what you mean Sam, but it's just that Alex hasn't gotten back to me and I sent her a congratulatory gift."

Samantha spoke slowly trying not to upset me. "Yeah, about that Charlie... I think it's best if you don't contact her again. And I mean that in the nicest possible way."

I cracked my knuckles. "I see what you mean Samantha."

Sam perked up. "You do? I mean that's great Charlie. So then you'll stop contacting her?" I paused, and Samantha thought I hung up on her. "Charlie?"

I cleared my throat. "Sure, sure, Sam. Actually, I just got a much better idea. I'll see you tomorrow! Don't be late! I'm going to need your help! Got to go."

Samantha yelled. "Charlie wait!"

I hung up the phone and took the bandages off my head. I needed a plan to win Alex's affection. I left work early and went to my barber for a trim. Then I bought a new black Prada suit, washed my Porsche and purchased two-dozen long stem pink roses and drove to Alex's boutique production company to win her heart. A friend of mine had done a little private eye work for me and clued me in on a few important details about Alex's life. Alex owned and operated a production house called LUCKY DUCK PICTURES. It was a boutique firm specializing in obscure and Independent films. My friend also informed me that Alex's phone had been ringing off the hook since she was released from jail. Every newspaper, magazine, morning and evening talk show wanted to hear her side of the story. She couldn't leave her house without being photographed by paparazzi. The attention Alex was receiving was creating a box office success out of her film, *Four Golden Stars*, though her private life was still in question. The public seemed unsure of how to react to Alex's violent outburst. While most papers agreed that I was a raging asshole, they couldn't condone Alex's crazy behavior. I was told Alex was mortified. She spent her time hidden in her office with the blinds lowered.

I pulled into Lucky Duck Pictures located in Chelsea and was met by a mob of paparazzi gathering outside her building waiting for Alex to do just about anything. They spotted me and like a pack of hungry wolves they rushed to my side, bombarding me with questions as I hurried toward the front door.

An attractive Latin woman in a navy blue tailored suit and slicked back hair came rushing towards me blocking me from entering the building. "Good afternoon Charlie. My name is Rachel and I'm from *Hollywood Magazine.* Can you tell us how you met Alex Rasner and why you gave her film, *Four Golden Stars,* such a bad review?" I paused. I was about to respond with a lewd remark, but then it hit me. I was in love and this was an opportunity to win Alex's affection, therefore I would tell this media hag anything she wanted to hear.

I looked the reporter straight in her emerald green eyes and said, "Do you mind," indicating that I would like my own microphone.

She seemed delighted as she handed me her microphone. "No, no not at all Mr. Evans!"

I took at deep breath. "I'll be happy to tell you why I gave her film such a bad review. It's simple, you see. I am an asshole. I get paid to be an asshole. Alex had every right to be mad at me, which is why I'm here with these roses in hopes of reconciling."

Rachel looked into the camera like she was reporting at some war torn village. "You're saying that you're here to apologize to Alex?"

I smiled. "That's right."

The reporter looked stunned. "You're not mad about the assault at your birthday party?"

My face turned red as I reiterated my thoughts, "I wouldn't say she assaulted me, so no… I'm not mad. I admire her. Now, if you'll excuse me I have to get in there and give these to her." I showed the camera the roses I was holding and handed the microphone back to the reporter. "I've got to go." Rachel moved out of my way as I bolted inside the building with several other reporters in tow.

Inside, an older heavy-set African American security guard with thick glasses was sitting at the front desk. I did my best to slide straight into the elevator before it shut, but I missed it by a second. As I turned around Earl greeted me.

"Hey." I said.

My private eye friend also informed me about Earl. He had been a security guard his whole life.

"You can't just go up. We… have to ca, ca, call… up first." Earl had a bad stutter, which was prime material for a man like me, but I bit my lip. I was determined to change my ways.

I smirked as I stared into Earl's chocolate brown eyes pretending like I didn't have a clue who he was. "What's your name, sir?"

Earl pulled his pants up and spoke with authority. "My name is Earl. Now th… the.. then, where di… di… did you sa… aay you were ge … going?"

I cocked my head. "I didn't. I'm here to see Alex Rasner." Earl put his hand on his chin like he was thinking.

"All ri...ri... right, she's on the fifteenth floor. Now just give me one minute."

Earl picked up the phone to call up to Lucky Duck Pictures as I slowly backed away from his desk and ran into the elevator waving goodbye to Earl as the door shut. Earl shuffled to the elevator and frantically pressed the elevator button, but it was too late. He ran back to his desk to alert Lucky Duck Pictures. When I stepped out of the elevator, Gary Clarkson was waiting for me. He looked unapologetic and bitter.

"What do you want Charlie?" I searched the quaint office decorated like a big Hollywood studio for Alex.

Alex was nowhere in sight, so I held my arms up. "I don't want any trouble. I just want to apologize to her. Where is she Mr. Clarkson?"

Gary guarded the front entrance like an English bulldog. "She's not here."

I peered around Gary. "I know you must have her tucked away in one of those tiny offices Gary; no one warned her that I was coming, so she couldn't have escaped." Seconds later, Alex emerged from hiding and I called out to her. "Alex!" I tried to dodge Gary, but he jumped in front of me. We went back and forth until I surrendered. "Okay, fine. Can you at least give these roses to Alex?" I wanted nothing more than to hold Alex in my arms as I stared at her from across the office. Gary stuck his hand out to take the long-stemmed roses letting down his guard.

"I'll make sure they're delivered to her doorstep."

I smirked, and then bolted around Gary and up to Alex who took one look at me and slammed her office door on my face repeatedly. I turned around slowly to face the rest of the office. "Okay. I guess she hasn't forgiven me yet. That's okay." I saw Earl step out of the elevator and I called out to him. "Earl! So glad you could make it. Your just in time to walk me out."

Earl turned to Gary who rolled his eyes and shook his head. "Get him out of here!"

Earl grabbed me by the arm. "Co... Co... come on, you."

I tried to persuade him to lighten up. "Is that really necessary? I'm leaving." I tried to tug my jacket from Earl's grip as I stepped into the elevator and stood shoulder to shoulder with him. As the elevator doors closed I cocked my head to the side and said, "By the way, has anyone ever told you that you are a lovely man?"

As the elevator doors opened in the lobby I peered out the window at the paparazzi waiting for me and I was struck by a brilliant idea. I turned to Earl. "Hey, you want to make this look good?" Earl looked confused. "Watch this." I showed Earl how to hold me by the collar so he could give me a proper bum's rush. Once Earl had a good hold of me I began to struggle and shout while Earl propelled me towards the door. I yelled out. "I've been kicked out of better places than this! Do you know who I am? Do you? This isn't over! Not by a long shot, buddy!" I gave Earl the sign of approval without letting the paparazzi catch wind of my victorious plan. The photographers snapped numerous pictures; they looked like they just struck gold as I yelled at the hapless security guard. I held my hand in front of my face, continuing the show as Alex opened the window of her fifteenth floor office and shouted, "Charlie!"

I looked up to see the roses soaring out the window as Alex glared down at me. Over the next few weeks several of my unsuccessful attempts to win Alex's affection were aired on the local news stations. I also ended up making the headlines, going viral on YouTube and racking up two million additional followers on Twitter and Facebook.

In *America Today*, there was a picture of Alex leaning her head out of her office window and dropping a box of chocolates on my head.

New York Daily Times: The *Angry Movie Guy* Just Won't Quit!

Morning News: Enough is Enough, *Angry Movie Guy!*

NY Daily Press: Just Quit While You're Ahead Snake!

Then there were the news crews. A petite blonde female reporter with a kick ass tan arrived on the scene ready to report.

"I'm standing outside of Lucky Duck Pictures waiting for the relentless *Angry Movie Guy* to be thrown out, yet again. For those of you watching at home who don't know whom Alex Rasner is. Alex is the writer and director of, *Four Golden Stars,* the movie everyone is raving about. Charlie "The Snake" Evans was beaten up and knocked down by Alex Rasner last week after he gave her one of the worst reviews in the history of his show. Ever since the ordeal, Charlie "The Snake" Evans, has made several attempts to apologize to Ms. Rasner, including today's effort where he strolled into the building wearing this ridiculous disguise." The camera crew's editor cut to an image of me wearing a long wig and dressed up like a hippie. Then, the editor cut back to the reporter. "Does he really think he's fooling any of us?" The reporter continued, "In just minutes we expect Rasner will throw whatever gift Charlie is trying to win her over with out the window." The camera faced Alex's window. Seconds later, the head of a teddy bear flew out the window and nearly missed a reporter as I came rushing out the front of Alex's building. The foxy female reporter yelled, "Here comes the Angry Movie Guy now!" I ran in front of the camera in the ridiculous get up and flashed the peace sign.

"Can't we just all get a long?" Then I picked up the head of the teddy bear and looked up at Alex. "Now that wasn't nice." I turned around and held up the head of the teddy bear to the camera. "What did that poor bear ever do to you?"

The blonde reporter announced, "I can't believe what I just witnessed female director, Alex Rasner just decapitated a stuffed teddy bear given to her by the *Angry Movie Guy!*"

The following day, Astral Charlie took some initiative and arrived at Alex's office ahead of me. He peered through Alex's office window. Alex flinched as Gary slammed the *NY Daily Times* down on her desk. "Well, we made the cover of the Daily Times." Alex picked up the newspaper.

NY Daily Times: It's a Match Made in Heave: The *Angry Movie Guy* and the even Angrier Movie Gal!

Astral Charlie pressed his face up against the window trying to read it. On the front cover there was a picture of Alex throwing a decapitated head of a teddy bear out the window. Alex took a deep breath.

"Okay that's it! When he shows up today, no matter what he does I'm not going to cause a scene. I'll just take whatever stupid gift he gives me and flush it down the toilet."

When Astral Charlie heard the good news he rushed back home to inform me. He flew up the stairs where I was finishing getting ready for work.

"Charlie, now's your chance. Make sure whatever gift you plan on giving her today is good! She can't toss it out the window like she did with all the rest!"

Later that day, when I showed up at Lucky Duck Pictures, Earl was prepared for me. He stood in front of the elevator with his arms crossed, convinced that there was no way in hell that I was going to get by him. One step forward, two steps backwards, three steps to the left and one quick dart to the right. I was in the elevator waving good-bye to a frustrated Earl.

"Can't we be friends Earl?"

Earl stammered. "You ba..ba.. bastard!"

Minutes later, I was deflated and being shown the door, but Astral Charlie stayed behind. He stared at Alex as she opened the gift I left her. Meanwhile, all the reporters had gotten used to our routine by now. They were waiting with their cameras pointed up at Alex's office window waiting for whatever gift I'd given her to come hurtling out the window, but nothing came flying out. The reporters looked at me.

"What can I say, I gave her a gift she couldn't refuse!"

Alex stared at the gift and became flushed with anger. "No, I can't keep it. That bastard!"

Astral Charlie tried to block the window. "You said you would flush it."

Alex walked over to the window with Gary trying to hold her back. "Alex you promised."

Alex shook her head. "I know. This is the last time, I swear!"

Gary sighed. "Fine!" Gary opened the window and yelled out. "Here it comes folks. Watch your heads!" And to my surprise the DVD I had given her came flying out the window.

Shocked by her lack of taste. I screamed, "Come on! It's an autographed copy of Star Wars! You know how long I had to harass George Lucas for that special edition?" The reporters looked at one another and then went scrambling for the DVD.

The following day, I decided to pay a visit to Dr. Bloom's office instead of going to give Alex the beautiful Chihuly vase I had picked out for her. When I walked into Dr. Bloom's waiting room, it was full of patients who immediately recognized me from the TV.

A little kid pointed at me. "Look it's that angry guy from the television."

I growled at the kid and his mother picked him up and carried him out of the waiting room. Then the other patients in the waiting room began to start pointing and whispering.

An old heavyset Caucasian man with a bruise over his forehead looked at the patient beside him and chuckled. "Look, that's the asshole from the T.V. show."

A skinny African American boy with a Mohawk looked up from his paper. "How does he even look at himself in the mirror?" They laughed. The African American boy continued, "I heard the television adds ten pounds, but he looks way fatter in person."

The old man added, "If I'd known he was a patient here I would have found a new Doctor a long time ago!"

"That's it!" I screamed, as I stood up in the middle of the waiting room and scowled at Dr. Bloom's patients. "At least I have a reason to be hated. What's your excuse? Is it your oversized ass that gets them or your bad haircut?" The old man and the skinny kid looked at one another and then left the waiting room in a huff. Then I turned around and dropped my trousers, mooning the rest of the mental patients and clearing out Dr. Bloom's waiting room.

When Dr. Bloom opened the door to his office he was shocked to see me. The private entrance of Dr. Bloom's office had been my saving grace. As a public figure, I didn't want to be seen coming and going from my therapist's office, but the door was locked this time. I stood up. "What? Do I have to call ahead every time? You've been watching the news haven't you? I'm in a crisis!"

Dr. Bloom let me in. "No, no, of course not Charlie. Come on in. Its just... do you know what happened to the other patients that were waiting?"

I shook my head. "I have no idea. Must have been something I said." I went into his office, sat down and then noticed that Dr. Bloom was dressed in women's clothes. I blinked my eyes a few times. "Doc, am I hallucinating or are you wearing pantyhose?"

Dr. Bloom tried to act normal. "No Charlie you are not hallucinating. I am wearing pantyhose and a woman's dress."

I stood up. "That's what I thought." I headed for the door, but Dr. Bloom stood up and blocked it. "I can explain Charlie, if you just give me a second."

I smiled. "I'm sure you can, but I'm not really interested. I've got enough on my plate right now."

Dr. Bloom looked concerned. "Please just give me a minute Charlie."

I squeezed my brow. "Fine." I muttered, as I stared at the floor trying not to make eye contact with Dr. Bloom, but then I noticed that Dr. Bloom was wearing pink pumps and I looked up.

Dr. Bloom breathed a sigh of relief as my eyes met his. "You see Charlie the patient that I was about to treat is going through an identity crisis and this is part of the therapy."

I nodded my head. "Uh-huh."

Dr. Bloom raised his voice. "I know it sounds a bit 'out there' Charlie, but it's a method and it has been working for him. So will you please have a seat and tell me what's on your mind?" Dr. Bloom pointed at the chair across from him. I tried to lighten the mood as I walked over to the chair to sit down.

"It's not that bad on you Doc, it's sort of like *Analyze this* meets *Priscilla Queen of the Desert*."

Dr. Bloom smiled. "Yes, I've been told that, but we're not here to talk about me. So tell me Charlie what's on your mind?"

I sighed and then began to tell Dr. Bloom my sad tale. "Well let's see. I've yet to come across a woman that doesn't end up despising me and when I finally do I give her the worst review in the history of mankind. Now she hates my guts."

Dr. Bloom grabbed his yellow pad to take notes. "Yes, that does pretty much sum it up Charlie. But what I want to know is… what are you going to do about it?"

I stood up and began to pace the room. "Haven't you been watching the news? I've tried to give her gifts, but she keeps chucking them out the window."

Dr. Bloom shook his head. "Yes, I know. It's such a shame."

"Tell me about it," I said, as I grabbed the rubber ball off Dr. Bloom's desk and squeezed it. "I feel drained." I moaned aloud, as I peered out Dr. Bloom's blinds. I wanted to make sure none of Dr. Bloom's patients had vandalized my Porsche.

Dr. Bloom stood up in his pink heels and walked over to where I was standing. "You just have to show her your true self Charlie. You need to be genuine with her. Don't try and win her over with gifts and trinkets. Do something that will show her the real you."

I grabbed my head. "My real self? You know what Dr. Bloom, I think you might be onto something." I snapped my fingers. "Of course! I've been trying to buy her love. Chicks don't want that. Well they do want that, but they want to feel something."

Dr. Bloom set his yellow pad down on his oversized mahogany desk. "Now you've got it Charlie."

I shook my head in agreement as I headed for the back exit. "If you don't mind Doc, I think I'm going to cut this appointment short."

Dr. Bloom smiled. "No problem, Charlie." Dr. Bloom stood up and walked to the back door like a pro in his pink pumps. I was about to open the door when Dr. Bloom stopped me. "By the way Charlie, if you ever want to wine and dine me you can?" I swallowed hard as I saw Dr. Bloom reach for the door; his fingernails were covered with long red press-on nails.

I tried to keep a straight face, but then I noticed something odd about Dr. Bloom's eyes. "Dr. Bloom, are you wearing mascara?"

Dr. Bloom winked and then purred. "Maybe he's born with it, or maybe it's Maybelline." I quickly dashed out the door as Dr. Bloom waived goodbye. "See you later Charlie."

I bolted out of Dr. Bloom's office and up to my Porsche. I knew this would be the last time I'd ever see Dr. Bloom in a professional setting, so I thought a parting gift was in order. I grabbed the vase out of the back seat and seconds later I peered through Dr. Bloom's back office window. I watched as he sat down in his chair and lit a cigarette. I'd finally discovered Dr. Bloom's secret. It was brilliant and twisted at the same time. I knocked on the back door of his office and ran back to my Porsche. I sat in the parking lot waiting for Dr. Bloom to open the door. I watched as he knelt down to pick up the Chihuly vase, admiring its beauty. It was nice to see his reaction. I wished Alex felt the same. Dr. Bloom looked around for the anonymous sender as I sped off in my Porsche honking my horn.

WHATEVER IT TAKES!

Chapter Twelve

"Whatever it takes, I'm willing to do it!" I screamed, as I rushed up the stairs to the photography studio where I had set up a high-profile photo session. I walked into a fully lit photography studio and was met by Misty, a butch looking female photographer covered in vintage tattoos. Misty immediately grabbed me by the arm and dragged me into makeup and hair. Forty minutes later, Misty stared at me through a long camera lens.

Misty had a thick Australian accent. "Now pull the cat closer to your face Charlie." I lifted up my cat Rexy and smiled at Misty who was doing her best to engage me in a polite conversation while taking my photograph. "It's really great that you found the time in your hectic schedule to pull this off Charlie. And to get all of these people on board… it's just marvelous!"

I smiled at the famous actors in the room. "I wanted to get involved in something I really care about Misty and if I can use my relationships to help a cause well… so be it."

Jake Durand, a tall, dark and handsome actor walked up to me while I was being photographed and sneered at me. "Your relationships? How did you describe one of my performances?"

I nervously chuckled. "Uh, I can't recall Jake."

Misty called out to Jake. "That's great Jake. Get in the picture. Why don't we have the two of you hold the cat together?"

Jake sneered at me. "Let me refresh your memory. You said, I couldn't act like I was on fire if you poured gasoline on me and struck a match."

I continued to smile for Misty. "Really? That was harsh of me? I thought I said that about the actor Howard Gontly."

Misty pulled the camera away from her eye. "Okay you two. You have to stop talking if you want these pictures to turn out. Charlie suck in your gut." Jake and I turned to the camera, smiled and the flash went off blinding us both.

Seconds later, the sexy screen siren, Jessica Moreau walked into the frame and stood on the opposite side of me. "Don't worry Jake. You want to know what he said about me?"

Jake smirked. "This ought to be interesting. Please…enlighten me Jessica."

Misty decided to keep snapping pictures regardless of our rude behavior. "Okay, everybody say cheese."

The two angry actors squeezed Charlie as they pretended to smile for the camera.

Jessica whispered. "He said my greatest contribution to cinema was going on hiatus to have my baby."

Jake snickered. "Wow! That's awful!"

I adverted my eyes from Jessica's sinister gaze. "I must have really been having a bad day Jessica. I'm sorry."

I could tell Misty was annoyed. She pulled the camera away from her face "Hey you guys, I'm not trying to be a downer, but you guys look angry in these pictures. How about we do a little less talking and a little more smiling. Remember it's for your furry friends."

I realized then that I hadn't completely thought this idea through. I waived to Misty to hold off for a minute. "Just give us one minute."

Misty put down her camera and picked up her pack of Camels. "Sure no problem, I've got all the time in the world. Don't mind me."

I turned towards Jake and Jessica with a sincere look of regret on my face. Jake and Jessica glared at me. I held my cat Rexy in front of me for protection. Jessica looked at Jake.

"Let me handle this one Jake."

But Jake was too irritated to let it go and went off on me. "I want to get one thing straight Angry Movie Dick, I mean Charlie. Jessica and I are here for the charity. Not for you!"

I waived the photographer back over. "I'm very clear about that and I appreciate it, believe me."

The photographer ordered us to focus on the shoot. "Okay, let's do this…. groups first and then we can shoot singles."

The three of us gathered into one seamless line and the photographer began to shoot. Once we were done we gathered around a laptop and inspected the day's shoot. The photos came out amazing. I was sure these would touch Alex's heart and save a few cats at the same time. "They're fantastic! Thanks everyone!"

Jake and Jessica glared at me and were about to insult me when my jaw dropped. I glanced at the television and to my surprise Eseray Knight, the morning talk show host was interviewing Alex.

Jake pointed to the television. "Hey, isn't that your little girlfriend who put you in the hospital?" Jessica and Jake gave one another a high five.

Jessica continued, "Yeah, she beat him up at his birthday!"

I glanced at them enjoying themselves and then back up at the T.V. "Someone turn up the volume!"

Misty's assistant searched for the remote.

I clamored for the remote. "Give it to me! Somebody turn it up. I can't hear it. Quiet!"

Jessica sneered, "Don't shush me."

My eyes narrowed. "I got to hear this Jessica, it's important."

The noise in the room subsided and Eseray could be heard speaking to Alex. She was holding Alex's hand. "Tell me Alex, how did it feel when you heard that review by Charlie 'The Snake' Evans, otherwise known as the *Angry Movie Guy*?"

Alex began to tear up. "It was devastating," she said brushing the tears from her cheek as she continued to win the audience over with her sad tale. "I put my heart and soul into that film. Not to mention every dollar I had to my name."

Eseray handed Alex a tissue. "Is that why you attacked Mr. Evans?"

Alex wiped the tears from her eyes. "I feel awful about doing that, but I can't take it back now. It's just something I'm going to have to live with. I was just so enraged! I made that film in honor of my mother who passed away when I was a little girl. It took a lot of strength for me to make that film and I guess when it was finished I felt like I'd somehow put her death to rest. When the *Angry Movie Guy* tore my film apart Eseray it felt like he ripped a whole in my heart all over again." Tears were now streaming down Alex's face.

Eseray put her hand on her chest. "I'm sorry for your loss Alex."

Alex smiled. "Thank you, Eseray."

Eseray stared into Alex's eyes. "One last question Alex before we go to a commercial break. Is it true that Mr. Evans has been contacting you since the event trying to apologize?"

Alex shook her head. "Yes Eseray. It's true. He has repeatedly come to Lucky Duck Pictures with flowers and candy. He even came with a signed *Star Wars* DVD. "Eseray Knight put her hand over her mouth like she was stunned. "He's been harassing my security guard and distracting my employees with his silly games. It's really inappropriate and I wish he would just stop."

Jake, Misty and Jessica all turned and stared at me. I picked up Rexy in his cat case and scurried towards the door. "Well, it was great working with all of you. Hope to do it again. Ciao!" I bolted toward the exit and standing near the doorway was Hollywood actors George Martinez and Brad Morel. I took one look at their menacing faces and decided there was no reason to stop and make amends. I rushed right passed them and out of the studio.

I missed the next two tapings of *Angry Movie Guy* and the producers were forced to play reruns for the first time in the history of the show. The whole crew expected today might be the same, but I showed up and dealt with Harry who gave me an ear full.

The door of Harry's office opened and the whole crew heard the end of Harry's hour-long speech. "Now quit screwing around Charlie and get out there and let's tape a show they will never forget!"

Harry slammed the door behind me. Being love struck did not make for a very good *Angry Movie Guy*. What was worse, is that the Chinese movie producers made a surprise visit to the studio, but I couldn't be bothered trying to impress the suits when Alex wouldn't give me the time of day.

Mr. Ho gave Harry a piece of his mind. "You better fix angry movie guy or this deal is off!"

The entire crew looked worried as I walked off the set sulking. I was headed to my dressing room until I spotted Samantha sitting on an apple box. I snuck up behind her like a giddy schoolboy and began to peer over her shoulder.

She was on the phone. "Front row seats? Sounds like a blast. Of course I'll be there! Count me in."

Samantha wrote down an event on her calendar. I squinted to read the location of the event, but she turned around to look at the clock and caught me lurking. "Ugh, I have to go. You know who is coming this way." Samantha stared at me like she was ready to kill me as she hung up the phone. I smiled trying to break the tension. Samantha faked a smile in return and said, "Can I help you?"

I went to sit down beside her on an empty apple box, but then stopped myself. "Can I sit here?"

Samantha tilted her head. "Do I have a choice?"

Shaking my head I said, "No, not really."

Sam scooted over. "Did you overhear anything interesting while eavesdropping on my private conversation?"

I played dumb. "What? Me? No…" I danced around her accusation and then changed the subject. "Listen, Samantha… I don't want to get you involved in my love affair. I just wanted to let you know I'm not some crazy stalker, even if I am kind of acting like one."

Sam stood up, taking me by surprise in her four inch red heels. "Yeah Charlie, you kind of are acting like a stalker."

I grabbed her hand and said, "I know. It's just that I want to talk to her, so I can explain how sorry I am. I need to express to her how I really feel."

Sam removed her hand from mine. "You've told her Charlie and she doesn't care."

I stood up shaking my head in denial, pleading with Samantha. "But she hasn't gotten to know the real me! The real Charlie!"

Samantha picked up her black nylon tote bag. "You didn't know her and that didn't stop you from trashing the one thing that mattered most to her."

I tried to stop Samantha from leaving. I was practically begging her to listen to my side of the story. "Your right Sam. I just wish there was a way I could make her listen. I want to make it better."

Samantha saw how desperate I seemed and for a moment I saw sympathy in her eyes. "I know you do. Believe me Charlie. But she is still so upset that she doesn't want to hear anything you have to say. So you might as well just save all your foolish attempts for someone else. And I mean that in the nicest possible way." Samantha turned to leave. "I have to go Charlie." Samantha headed for the studio doors leading to the parking lot. She was practically at her car when I burst out of the doors with her organizer in my hand.

"Samantha...wait!"

Samantha turned around startled. "What is it?"

"Here!"

Samantha grabbed the organizer from my hand. "Oh my god, my whole life is in this thing. I'd be lost without it. Thanks Charlie." Sam got into her mini-cooper, "I have to run Charlie. Have a good weekend." I waived goodbye as Sam sped off with her window rolled down blaring the song, *I got moves like Jagger*, by Maroon 5. "See you soon!" She honked her horn.

I smiled deviously. "Sooner than you think." I had "accidentally" gone through Samantha's organizer and discovered where her and Alex would be partying over the weekend. I rushed to my Porsche and headed to La Mystique. I made my way through the crowded bar and sat down at Harry's regular seat waiting for Sean to appear. Sean strutted out of the kitchen and was taken by surprise to see me there without my normal "bodyguard" and his blonde table accents. I could tell by the way he was strutting up to the table that he wasn't in the mood for any of my insults. I jumped out of the booth and stepped in front of him. "Sean, can I talk to you for a second?"

Sean looked me dead set in the eyes. "A second is way too long to put up with you."

Sean tried to walk off, but I stopped him. "You're one of those singing, dancing, acting kind of… guys" I wiggled my fingers like a little fairy. "Right?"

Sean looked aghast as he put his hands on his hips. "The term you are looking for is triple threat. Seven years of interpretive dance, eight years of Stella and four years at the Round About, thank you very much." Sean snapped his fingers emphasizing his accomplishments.

"Wow! I said, "And five years here getting my drink orders. Well, I'm glad to see that's working out for you."

Sean turned his back on me. "I've had enough of this shit chat Charlie. Do you want a drink or what?"

I held my hand up. "I'm sorry. Listen, I need your help."

Sean turned around and glared at me. "Why would I help you?"

I struggled with the words. "Because I need someone with your… expertise."

Sean held up his hands and looked at his nails. "Really? That must suck for you."

I walked in front of Sean. "It does actually."

Sean folded his arms. "Well don't worry."

I looked stunned. "Seriously?"

Sean raised his eyebrows. "Yes, because I would never help you for any reason under the sun."

I handed Sean a piece of paper. "Look, I just need you to show up at this place and time for maybe fifteen minutes."

Sean let out a snort of disgust. "You can't afford me."

I stared at Sean. "There is three thousand cash in it for you and I'll buy your drinks."

Sean grabbed the piece of paper out of my hand. "What will you be wearing because I wouldn't want to clash?" He grinned and jumped up and down.

I sighed with relief. "Perfect. I'll see you there. Don't be late and don't stand me up."

Sean waived goodbye to me holding the note in his hand. "Wouldn't think of it!"

The next morning I woke up panicked, feeling like I'd wasted my entire life on a show that left me without a friend in the world.

Trying to relax, I popped *Lost in Her Eyes* into the DVD player. I continued watching from where I'd last left off. Edie Greene appeared on the T.V. screen wearing a long navy blue dress with a tiny belt wrapped around her slim waste accentuating her curvaceous body. She'd strolled into the nightclub for a quick nightcap hoping to calm her nerves. Her brother had gotten himself into yet, another jam and needed money. Edie sat down at the bar and glanced at the crowd of people in the club.

To her surprise, Jack was snuggled up with a young brunette at a secluded table. Edie tried not to stare until she realized it was her friend. She had set the two of them up weeks ago and now Jack was out on a second date with her. Edie ordered herself a scotch on the rocks and tried to blend in with the crowd. She didn't want Jack to notice her now that she knew he was on a date.

Edie thought to herself…why wouldn't Jack tell me that he was having a second dinner date with Ivy? I would have persuaded him not to go. Could he be falling in love with her?" Edie watched as Ivy twirled her hair between her fingers. Edie muttered, "Ugh! Why is she laughing so much? Jack isn't that funny!"

Jack looked up from his conversation and to his surprise he noticed Edie sitting at the bar. He couldn't believe his stroke of luck. Asking the pretty dame on a second date was his way of testing Edie's true feelings for him. He told himself, "To drop to his knees and propose marriage to Edie if she shows any sign of jealousy." Jack knew that he would never find a more suitable match. Now, with Edie at the nightclub he wouldn't have to wait for days till the news traveled to her. He could test his theory right then and there. Jack leaned in closer to Ivy and grabbed her by the hand. Then he deliberately whispered something clever into her ear. Ivy began to laugh even harder. Jack stood up nonchalantly and asked Ivy to dance. Edie tried not to watch. She didn't want to appear to be eavesdropping, but she couldn't help herself. She leaned on the bar and called out to the bartender.

"Bailey!"

Bailey turned to Edie with a huge smile on his face. "How can I help you Edie?"

Edie set her glass down. "May I have another round dear?"

Bailey picked up the glass. "Anything for you sweetheart."

Edie blushed and put her hand on Bailey's. "Oh Bailey, I was wondering if you would be a dear and tell me if Jack's here?" She hoped that Bailey would spill the beans on how long Jack's date had been going on.

Bailey pointed to where Jack had been sitting. "He's been sitting all night with that pretty little lady he's dancing with now. I think they make a magnificent couple, don't you?"

Edie faked a smile. "Lovely."

Watching her friend flirt with Jack Waters was making her nauseous. She'd only set them up on a date because she felt sorry for the girl and now Jack was swinging her around the dance floor like she was a little doll on heels. Edie sauntered to the back of the bar and up to the piano player.

She tapped Bill on the shoulder. "I'd like to sing something if you don't mind Bill."

Bill smiled, showing off his big set of pearly whites for Edie. "Sure, anything for you, Edie."

Edie blushed. "Thank you, dear. I think I'll sing something a little jazzy." Bill finished his set and the crowd joyously clapped, as Jack did one last twirl, dipping Ivy. Ivy tilted her head back and noticed that Edie was standing on the stage. She motioned to Jack to lift her back up. As they walked back to the table Ivy turned to Jack seductively.

"You didn't tell me Edie would be here tonight?"

Jack stared at Edie on the stage. "I would have if I'd known, but I'm just as surprised as you are." They sat down and watched as Edie seductively approached the microphone and began to sing a song by an unknown artist titled, 'Go Tease Someone Else'. The jazzy number was so hot and sizzling that the whole audience began to blush as Edie swayed through the room locking eyes only with Jack as she worked the crowd.

"Go tease someone else, 'cause I won't be around. I'm going to get myself up and get right out of town."

Jack practically melted at the sound of Edie's voice and began speaking to himself, completely forgetting his surroundings and his company. "I think I might just have died and gone to heaven."

Ivy looked over at Jack staring at Edie in awe and she knew his words were not meant for her. By the time Edie got back into the bar area Jack was alone and waiting for her. The club was dying down and soft jazz music played in the background of the candle lit room. There was sparse chattering amongst the remaining guests. Edie walked up to the bartender and ordered another drink as Jack casually slid up beside her. "I didn't expect to see you here."

Edie grabbed her drink and turned to Jack. "I didn't expect to see you here either. Where's Ivy?"

Jack smiled. "She went home."

Edie looked at herself in her compact mirror. "So early?"

Jack chuckled. "Well, I think it was past her bed time."

Edie batted her eyes. "Oh, that's too bad. You two seemed like you were having such a good time."

Jack took a drink, hesitating just long enough to get under Edie's skin before he replied, "I was."

Edie twirled her hair between her fingers. "Really? Do tell?"

Jack smirked. "Isn't it impolite for a man to reveal his feelings about one woman to another woman?"

Edie turned to Jack. "Not if that woman set you up with that woman."

Jack smiled at Edie. "Really? Is that the way it works?"

Edie smiled and Jack swooned in his chair. "What do you want to know?"

Edie bit her bottom lip as if she was thinking of the perfect question. Then she looked at Jack coyly and asked, "Is she a good kisser?"

Jack chuckled. "That's very presumptuous of you to think that I might have already kissed her."

Edie pulled her lipstick out of her purse and began to apply the red-hot lipstick. "Well didn't you?"

Jack could tell where Edie was leading him. "Yes, but that isn't why I decided to ask her out on a second date."

Edie snapped her purse shut. "Oh really? Then what was the reason?"

Jack took a sip of his bourbon and then smiled at Edie. "I had a good time."

Edie sort of furrowed her brow. "You had a good time?"

Jack laughed. "Yes. Wasn't that the point?"

Edie looked away. "Sure it was the point." Edie pointed to the bartender to top off her drink. Jack did the same.

"You seem upset Edie."

Edie's hair dropped in front of her face and she didn't remove it. "I do not. Why would I be upset?"

Jack reached over and tucked Edie's hair behind her ear. "You tell me?"

Edie looked away. "It's my brother. He's in trouble. That's why I came here. I couldn't sleep. I was worried about him Jack." Jack immediately became concerned and felt foolish for insinuating otherwise. "I'm sorry Edie. Is there anything that I can do for you?"

Edie eyes filled with tears. "No, I don't think so. I just didn't want to be alone, that's all. I thought you might be here and then when I saw you with my friend, I must admit it made me a bit jealous."

Jack looked hopeful. "Oh really? So that's why you decided to sing that little number. You wanted to break up the fun?"

Edie wiped the tears from her eyes. "Well I didn't think she would leave. Why did she decide to leave Jack?"

Jack swiveled his chair towards Edie. "She left because I might have mentioned that I thought I died and gone to heaven when you sang."

Edie turned away blushing. "You didn't say that to her? Did you?"

Jack nodded his head. "I did. I didn't mean to. I meant to just think it, but my thoughts were louder than I expected. The next thing I knew Ivy was up on her feet and headed towards the exit. I guess she figured I must have feelings for you."

I sighed to myself, pathetically crying like a woman as I watched Edie and Jack's relationship blossom on the T.V. screen. I wanted the same thing. I whined, "Why couldn't it be me?

206

Haven't I suffered enough?" Rex climbed on top of me purring loudly as if to say, "You are not alone Charlie." I grabbed Rexy. "At least you love me Rexy." Rex purred louder. He was hungry and insistent about being fed. I sniffled. "Wait a minute Rexy! This is my favorite part." I turned up the sound.

Edie turned to Jack. "Well you'll just have to clear it up with her when you see her tomorrow." Jack shook his head no.

Edie's eyes fluttered. "Why not?"

Romantic music began to play in the background. Jack grabbed Edie's hands and gazed deep into her eyes. "Because, every time I see you I get lost in your eyes."

Edie gasped, "You do?"

Jack smiled. "It's like being on a wonderful endless road or staring into the stars when I'm with you Edie." The romantic music ended abruptly.

Edie pulled her hands away. "Oh Jack. I didn't know that you felt that way."

Jack stared into her eyes like he was trying to penetrate her soul. "How could you not know? I only agreed to go out with those other women so I could get close to you Edie. They mean nothing to me. But you insisted I find love when I'd already found it. Only the woman I was in love with wouldn't have me."

Edie turned away. "Don't tease me Jack."

Jack looked stunned. "Oh is that what that song was all about? You think I'm teasing you? You think that I don't mean what I say?" The romantic music began to play again. "I do mean it Edie, every word of it. I am in love with you Edie Greene. I finally know love is not just a chemical reaction going off in the brain. It's something much deeper than that. I've never felt this way, not in my entire life and I know I will never feel this way about any other woman ever again!"

Edie's eyes widened, "You're actually serious?"

"Of course I'm serious." Jack dropped to his knees and pulled a gorgeous ring out of his pocket. He put it on Edie's finger.

"Edie Greene will you marry me and make me the happiest man in the world?"

Edie appeared stunned. "Where did that ring come from?"

Jack shook his head. "Don't worry about it, Edie. Will you marry me?"

Edie jumped up, beaming with joy. "Yes, yes! I will marry you. I love you Jack Waters. I believe I loved you since the day I laid eyes on you. Only I didn't know that love could be this real." Edie held up her finger to stare at the ring. Then she joyously spun around. "It's beautiful Jack Waters!" Jack leaned in and passionately kissed Edie.

The following morning Edie woke up in Jacks arms. She held her hand out to admire her ring. "You never did tell me where it came from?"

Jack leaned over and kissed Edie tenderly. "Does it really matter?"

Edie snuggled up to Jack, taking in the scent of his cologne. "I'm just curious, that's all. Bragging rights are in order."

Jack gave Edie another kiss. "Okay. It was my mother's ring. It was locked away in the safe for God knows how long until last week when I decided to have the jewelers look at it." Jack pointed out the new diamonds added to the ring. "Of course, while I was there I decided to have a few new diamonds added. It needed to be as perfect as you are."

Edie sat up, looking as beautiful as she did the night before. "So you've been planning this?"

Jack smiled coyly. "Let's just say I didn't think there would be a third date with Ivy." Jack pulled a paper out from his bedside drawer. It was the list of woman Edie had arranged for him to go out with. He showed it to her. There was a big heart around Edie's name. "See… you were next on the list. I had to be prepared."

Suddenly, an overwhelming sense of anxiety consumed me. I began to tear up. "I can't do it! She's going to laugh at me." I sprang up from the couch, knocking Rexy off my lap. I turned off the movie with the remote and began to pace. I was second-guessing my plans for the evening. I went to the phone and to my surprise I called Harry for help. The phone rang and rang. Harry finally answered the phone. I could hear his Jacuzzi jets bubbling in the background. "Hello? Harry? Harry!"

I could hear Harry speaking to someone. "I'm going to make you a star. You just wait and see! But we got to do something about that last name of yours… Sminkler! You sound like a Smurf."

I screamed into the phone. "Harry! Stop trying to hump your neighbor's daughter. She's too young for you!"

Harry finally answered me. "Charlie?"

I sighed. "Yeah, it's me. I have a favor to ask you."

"A favor?" Harry snorted.

I'd never asked Harry for anything, but things were different now. I was desperate.

"Well go on Charlie."

I took a deep breath. "It's pretty simple Harry. All I need you to do is to bring a couple of hot women to a place I'm going to be at tonight."

Harry began to laugh and his neighbor began to giggle in unison. "Is that all?"

I paused. "Almost...."

Harry hissed. "I'm listening Charlie."

I stuttered. "The... then you have to let me sing to one of them to make another girl jealous." I could hear Harry step out of the Jacuzzi. I wanted to hang up as I listened to him flirt with the prepubescent pre-Madonna that lived next door to him. I imagined Harry tickling the behind of the girl while adjusting his gigantic boner, until he finally interrupted my paranoid nightmare with a high-pitched shriek

"Well, hot doggie! I'm in. I can't wait to get your mind off that clown who's been bringing my show down. So who's the lucky lady?"

I paused. "Uh... it's her Harry. It's Alex I'm trying to make jealous."

I listen to Harry take off his hat and hit the side of his leg like he always does when he's pissed. "Now either you're just plain stupid or you're just plain stupid. Haven't you learned anything by now? Nothing you do is going to get through to that girl!"

I felt elated and miserable at the same time. "This is my last try Harry and then I'm going to throw in the towel and go back to being my miserable shallow old self."

I could almost see the look of joy on Harry's face as he answered me. "Now that's what I like to hear. Alright, sign me up!"

I sighed heavily. "There's just one other thing."

Harry seemed annoyed. "What?"

"I just thought I should mention that Sean, the waiter from La Mystique, will be joining me."

Harry laughed so hard he almost choked. "No shit! How in the hell did you convince him to do a thing like that?"

I was beginning to feel encouraged again. "I told him I would pay him three grand and buy all his drinks. He agreed without batting an eye. He even offered to call me first to make sure we don't clash." I waited as Harry moved from the Jacuzzi to the kitchen. I listened to him blend a frozen drink.

"Hot damn! Let's get the show on the road!"

I sighed. "Alright, but make sure the girl is hot Harry, but not bimbo hot and not under age! She needs to appear wholesome enough to make Alex jealous." I went to my closet and pulled a box off the top shelf. I removed a fedora that looked exactly like Jack Water's.

Harry stopped the blender. "I'm on it Charlie. I know the perfect duo for tonight's show." I heard Harry open the sliding glass door and return to the pool. He ignored me as he sat down handing Sminkler a cocktail. "Here you go doll! Why don't you go back to the Jacuzzi while I finish up on my call." I listened to Harry smack her behind. "That's a good girl." I was becoming agitated while listening to Harry flirt with the teenage neighbor he had been bragging about all summer.

I felt like I should do something to stop him. "Harry! Harry!" Harry chimed in. "Don't worry Charlie. I will be there tonight with two hot tamales and I guarantee you at least one of them will make everyone in the room think she is madly in love with you."

I sighed with great relief. "Great!"

I hung up the phone and went back into my walk-in closet to pick out a slick suit. I needed one that made me look and feel like Robert Palmer singing, "Simply Irresistible." After changing twenty-some odd times I regrettably headed to the Karaoke bar.

I walked into an almost empty lounge in Manhattan's Korea town. It was dimly lit and had a disco ball on the ceiling above an old stage in the center of the room. A drunk Asian female was singing *Bad Romance*, by Lady Gaga off-key. I had asked Sean to arrive a little early so we could grab a drink together. I found him seated in the back of the lounge sipping on his second Long Island ice-tea. He waived me over. "Charlie!" As I moped over to his table I noticed he looked quite dapper in a dark Ralph Lauren blazer and navy blue Levi's. I sat next to Sean and he began pestering me right away. "So what's the story with this girl anyway? She beats you up at your own birthday and now you want to like marry her?"

I gazed at Sean with peculiar familiarity. "How did you know that I want to marry her?"

Sean shook his head. "Charlie, I'm actually scared for you."

I replied. "Don't be. I know you think I'm some sick sadistic son of a bitch who gets beat up by women." Sean nodded his head in agreement. "But actually I'm a really nice guy with feelings for a girl who only sees me as a sadistic son of a bitch, and if I don't convince her otherwise… she's going to walk out of my life and into the arms of God-knows who!"

Sean took a large gulp of his long island ice-tea. "You do realize she hates your guts, right? It's all over Page 6."

I rolled my eyes. "Thanks Sean. I'm not a complete moron… no matter how it may appear to anyone. Yes, I do realize she wants nothing to do with me, but I know she must find it somewhat romantic that I keep trying. I was relentless and because of it her film turned into an overnight success."

Sean flicked his nails. "You knew that would happen if you kept making a scene in front of her building with the paparazzi?"

I pursed my lips. "Yes, but that's not the only reason why I did it. I mean…I do have feelings for her, as strange as it may seem to everyone else."

Sean sighed, "Aw, Charlie's in love. I'm kind of feeling guilty now about taking your money."

I put my hand out. "You can give it back."

Sean snorted. "I'm not feeling that guilty. I need some new Prada in my life. Now tell me what I need to do."

I put my arm around Sean and walked him to the back of the bar. "Okay, so Harry is on his way here with a beautiful woman who is going to pretend to adore me as we sing the song I chose."

Sean pulled away from me. "Wait... I thought it was Alex that you are pining over?"

I nodded my head. "It is."

Sean put his hand up. "Then why are we going to sing to this other girl?"

I put my arm back around Sean. "Well if you just let me finish, you would understand."

Sean nodded his head. "Fair enough, continue."

I eagerly revealed my half-witted plan to win Alex's heart. "So…you are going to notice Alex sitting in the front row and point her out to me and then I'm going to be torn between the two incredibly gorgeous women, eventually choosing Alex and winning her over with my song and dance moves."

"I see?" Sean said, as he looked away.

I stared at the back of Sean's head waiting for him to turn around. I rolled my eyes. "What is it?"

Sean looked at me for a second and then turned away again. "No, nothing."

I backed away. "You think it's a stupid idea, don't you?"

Sean took a deep breath. "I've heard better. To be honest, it sounds like you've been watching too many B-movies Charlie."

I was agitated by Sean's obnoxious comment. "Well do you have a better idea?"

Sean rolled up his sleeves and contemplated it for a second. "Let's see... hmm, nope I'm blank." A cute waitress walked over and Sean flagged her down. "Waitress. Can you get us another round of drinks?"

She smiled and said, "Sure thing."

Sean handed the waitress a twenty I'd given to him earlier. I stood up and walked away holding my stomach.

Sean howled. "Where are you going?"

I frowned. "I feel nauseous."

Sean looked at me disgusted. "You're not going to blow chunks on stage, are you?"

I mimicked Sean's annoying voice. "No. I'm not going to blow chunks on stage. I'm just a bit queasy."

I began to walk away, bent over in pain.

Sean called after me. "Hey Charlie! What song are we singing?"

I turned around, paused and then said with the straightest face I could muster, "Total Eclipse of The Heart!"

Sean nearly choked on his long island ice-tea. "Really…I mean nice choice."

I walked back over to where Sean was sitting annoyed and flustered. "Just forget about helping me, alright? I'll do this thing on my own."

Sean sat down, his eyes gleaming with revenge. "By all means, I'll just sit and watch, but I'm keeping the three grand for brushing my teeth and putting on my best pair of denim."

I hollered at him. "Fat chance sister!"

Sean sat up and turned around and tapped his ass. "You want some of this big boy?"

I tried to cover my face with my jacket. "Stop it! You're causing a scene."

Sean wiggled his butt. "I know you do!" Sean slapped his ass again.

I looked at him disgusted. "I'm going to vomit." I could have gone back and fourth with Sean all night, but I noticed the room filling up and I began to panic. I rushed off yelling at Sean, "I've sacrificed everything for love! And I'd do it again. Now get ready to perform!"

A crowd of people stared at Sean as his face turned beat red from anger. "What? Serves him right." Sean whipped his head around so fast it almost fell off.

The second I scurried off Harry strutted into the Karaoke bar with a couple of hot women suctioned cupped to his side. He was wearing a white button down Polo dress shirt, black Armani slacks and a red tie. "Hey Sean! Where's Charlie?"

Sean turned around and saw Harry. He rolled his eyes. "He's in the bathroom puking."

Harry didn't bat an eye. "Great! Well, meet Hailey and Nina. They are two friends of mine from out of town here to help Charlie out."

Sean raised his glass. "Nice to meet you. So which one of you is the one I'm supposed to help Charlie seduce and then publicly diss?" A tall redhead with big green eyes raised her hand. "Hi, I'm Hailey." Sean batted his eyes at Hailey and then made a sarcastic remark. "You must be so proud."

Harry hit Sean. "Cut it out, would ya?"

Sean looked at Harry annoyed, "What's in it for me?"

Harry glared at Sean. "I thought Charlie was paying you?"

Sean put out his hand. "He is, but..."

Harry rolled his eyes. "Say no more." He reached into his pocket and pulled out a hundred dollar bill and two tickets to the Broadway show, *Kinky Boots*. He whispered to Sean. "I had planned on giving the tickets to the girls, but I guess."

Sean pocketed the hundred and the two tickets. "You made the right decision."

Meanwhile, I was in the bathroom giving myself a necessary pep talk. I breathed deeply as I leaned over the sink trying not to vomit. "You can do this Charlie."

Astral Charlie flew out from one of the stalls. "It stinks like piss in here." Astral Charlie looked around the room trying to get his bearings straight. "No wonder! What are you doing here Charlie?" I looked into the mirror. I was wearing a top hat, a fake mustache and carrying a walking stick. Astral Charlie looked shocked. "Don't tell me you are planning on wearing that Charlie? You are going to make a fool out of me."

I straightened my tie and cracked a smile. "Now I feel like Jack Waters." I walked out of the bathroom a few minutes later and spotted Harry sitting with Sean and two beautiful women. "Here goes nothing."

Astral Charlie flew after me screaming. "Stop Charlie! I've heard you sing in the shower! You're going to make a complete ass out of yourself!"

I imagined what Jack Waters must have felt like walking through his nightclub while everyone stared at him. I strutted up to the table noticing heads turning in my direction. I spotted Alex and to my surprise she was pointing me out to one of her friends. It was obvious that she had no clue that it was I, but my heart still skipped a beat. I muttered, "It's working!" I approached the table where Sean was sitting with Harry and the girls. Sean nearly split his pants at the sight of me in my ridiculous get up.

I whispered loudly. "Would you shut up? Everyone is looking." I thought I was going to have to call the whole thing off as I watched people at the next table begin to point and stare.

I heard a girl whisper, "Who's that?" Her friend responded, "Who knows... probably some wannabe showing off for his friends."

Harry stood up and handed Sean another hundred. "Now cool it! You're here to help, not to impersonate a laughing hyena."

I looked at Harry stunned. "Thanks, Harry."

Harry smiled. "Of course. What are friends for? Come sit down Charlie." I went and sat next to Harry and was introduced to a beautiful redhead named Hailey. Harry stood up, "I'm going to grab some drinks. Why don't you get to know the ladies Charlie?"

I stood up and tapped Harry on the shoulder. "Thanks for doing this Harry." Harry smiled and then walked away. The women Harry had brought with him were definitely a couple of knockouts. Hailey was beautiful enough to make any woman jealous. I started laying it on pretty thick, hoping to impress Hailey and her friend. I wanted to make her laugh so that Alex would look over. Sure enough... a few big laughs from Hailey and I had Alex's attention. It was happening just like it had for Jack in *Lost in Her Eyes*.

Sean noticed what was happening and couldn't believe his eyes. "It's working Charlie. She's looking at you." Sean encouraged Hailey's friend Holly to join in. "Come on! Let's make her drool over Charlie." Holly pulled her chair in closer and began to laugh; they all clinked glasses.

Meanwhile, Harry had snuck away and taken it upon himself to get the publicity involved. He was huddled in the corner of the Karaoke bar making phone calls to the press. Harry wanted the whole thing caught on camera. 'The Angry Movie Guy Sings His Heart Out To The Even Angrier Movie Gal'. Harry knew he needed to do something to convince Mr. Ho that my set back was only a temporary one. Later I learned, Harry had told Mr. Ho all I needed was to have my heart broken by Alex and I would be angrier than ever. He supposed, "Once this is over, Charlie will be willing to write reviews that will rip the hearts out of children."

Harry returned to the table with a waitress holding a round of drinks and discreetly announced, "It's almost show time folks. Everyone grab a shot because like it or not Charlie is about to sing his desperate heart out." Harry handed me a shot of tequila. I looked at it and shook my head.

Sean immediately grabbed it and downed it. "I'll take it." Then Sean pulled me away from the girls. "Come here Charlie. I want to talk with you." Sean tried to persuade me to reconsider my courageous gesture. "Why are you doing this Charlie? Couldn't you just find some starry eyed bimbo who didn't see right through you to screw and save every one a lot of bother?"

Hailey and Holly tried to listen as I held Sean by the shoulders. "I paid you three grand to do this Sean so, I think you have a right to know."

Sean hiccupped. "Know what?"

I took a deep breath. "The thing is Sean I don't want some starry eyed bimbo. You've known me for years, right?"

Sean hiccupped. "Sadly, yes."

"And I've always been an asshole that entire time, correct?"

Sean shook his head yes. "Indubitably."

"But that's not who I am Sean. And when I met Alex I remembered that. Only because I've been acting like an asshole, she won't give me the time of day. Ironic, huh?"

Sean put his hand on his hip. "Yeah, women are funny that way." The two ladies listened to me as I poured my heart out to Sean and they actually began to feel sorry for me.

Hailey touched my hand. "So you've been doing all of these things just to talk with her?"

I nodded my head. "Yeah, that's the long and short of it."

Sean looked at me differently. "There might be a soul in there after all Charlie."

I smiled at Sean and then looked at him perplexed. "You think? Chicks like that, don't they? Souls? Heartfelt emotion and honesty and all that junk?"

Sean straightened my tie. "Yes, darling. They eat it up with a spoon. But don't call these ladies chicks, all right? Only other women and gay men can do that."

Suddenly a loud scream broke up our conversation. Samantha had arrived and all the girls were excited to see her. "Sorry I'm late. I hope you didn't sing, 'Like a Virgin' with out me."

Alex laughed and signaled for a waiter. "We wouldn't dream of it."

I pointed Samantha out to Holly and Hailey. "That's my assistant on my show. Alex is her cousin."

Sean looked at me astonished, "No way!"

I smiled. "Yep! It's fate. The stars brought us together and they will rip us apart if I don't figure out a way to fix this situation." The ladies at my table began to sigh.

Holly put her hand on her heart. "That is so sweet."

Hailey put her arms around me. "You can count on me to be completely seduced and then thoroughly destroyed when you choose Alex."

Just then a bartender walked up to me and tapped me on the shoulder. "You're up."

I nodded okay. "Let's do this." I walked onto the stage terrified by what I was about to do.

Sean looked at me as he stumbled onto the stage. "Smile, suck in your gut and what ever you do... don't look them in the eyes." I tried to shake it off. "Don't worry," he said, "You'll bring down the house."

I approached the microphone just as I saw Jack do it in, *Lost in Her Eyes*. "This one is for someone special in the room. A woman, who when I see her...I get lost in her eyes." And then the lights went down and the music came up. Sean and I began to belt out the lyrics to Jim Steinman's, "Total Eclipse of the Heart."

"Turn around... Every now and then I get a little bit lonely and you're never coming around... Turn around..."

I watched as Samantha's mouth dropped open. "Oh my God. Is that Charlie? Why is he here? What is he doing? What is he wearing? Who is that woman he's singing too?" Hailey was at one end of the stage swooning over me when Sean pointed to Alex on the opposite side. I peered into Alex's eyes, took off my top hat and then slid across the stage landing directly in front of Alex singing, "Every now and then I get a little bit tired of listening to the sound of my tears... Turn around bright eyes... Every now and then I fall apart! And I need you now tonight!" Alex stood up, unsure of what to do as both Sean and I belted out the remaining lyrics of the song. "And I need you more than ever! And if you only hold me tight we'll be holding on forever! And we'll only be making it right, because we'll never be wrong!"

Alex's look of bewilderment quickly turned into frustration as she bolted out of the lounge while Karaoke fans snapped pictures of both her and I.

Astral Charlie flew out after Alex. I handed the microphone to Sean and ran after her as well. To my surprise the paparazzi were outside waiting for us and began snapping photos nonstop.

I yelled out. "Can't we just talk? If you'll just let me talk with you I know..."

Alex turned around. "There is nothing I want to say to you and there is nothing you can say to me to change my mind Charlie. You are a shallow, vacuous, horrible man. You are truly a snake!"

I screamed. "But that's not really me! You don't know me. Not yet, anyway."

Alex walked up to me. "And you don't know me. You chase me all over town with your pathetic attempts to try and win me over."

I smiled at her. "They weren't all pathetic, were they? I mean, I thought that was pretty good in there."

Alex shook her head no. "You know what's really sad?"

I looked defeated. "What?"

Alex proclaimed, "That you do all this, the gifts, the singing and the tracking me down all to get to know me. When all you had to do was watch my movie."

I put my hands in the air. "I did!"

Alex yelled, "No, no Charlie. You didn't. If you'd really seen it and hated it I could respect that. But you trashed it because it's second nature to you at this point. And you want to know something else?" I looked hopeful. "Anything you'd ever want to know about me is in that film. All you had to do was look." Alex backed away from me. "Good night Charlie, and good bye!"

And just like that Alex walked away leaving me standing alone in the parking lot with the photographers flashing photos. The night had turned into the worst night of my life. I raced home, flipped on the stereo and poured myself a scotch. I plopped down on the sofa as the song; "I only have eye's for you," by the

Flamingo's played. I began to sulk. I couldn't remember the last time I felt so horrible.

Astral Charlie floated above me. He was almost as depressed as I was. "I thought she would have come to her senses by now Charlie, but some people just don't know what's good for them even if it hits them over the head." "It's not your fault!" He exclaimed, "You can lead the horse to the water, but sometimes no matter what you do the horse won't drink."

I picked up an old photo album sitting on my coffee table and began to flip through it. I opened it to a picture of my mother and began to ball my eyes out. "I'm sorry Mom. Your little boy managed to mess things up pretty bad." I slumped down into the sofa and cried myself to sleep.

The next morning I woke up to an angry pounding at my door. I walked to the door with my eyes half shut and holding my aching head. To my surprise, my father was standing outside my front door.

I barked, "What the hell are you doing here?"

Ray looked almost as deflated as I did. "You don't answer your father's phone calls anymore, so I had to come to you."

Looking around outside I muttered, "How the hell did you get in here?"

My father shrugged his shoulders. "I've been in the real estate business for thirty-five years I know a few people in the doorman union."

I gave him a strange look and then said, "Crackers! That's just crackers! I buy a three point five million dollar condo and you get in with a twenty dollar bill."

My father stood at the entryway waiting for me to invite him in. "Give me some credit Charlie. I handed him a C-Note. Now are you going to show some pity on your old man and invite me in or…"

I moved out of the way. "Well are you coming in or not?" My father took off his hat and set in on the table. "To what do I owe this great pleasure?" I stared at my father waiting for a response. I was stunned by his appearance. He looked old and depressed.

"It's Yasmine. She's leaving me."

I smirked. "Really? She always seemed to be so loyal. The epitome of character."

My father began to cough and I noticed he had to sit down in order to catch his breath. "Your sarcasm is not appreciated Charlie. Save that act for your show. I'll have you know she was a good girl. I wasn't. But for her to leave me is still ridiculous. We had an understanding."

I laughed. "What was that? You pay her credit cards every month in exchange for a don't tell policy about your nineteen year old intern?"

Ray glared at me. "Don't be a smart ass. The intern is twenty-two and I paid way more than Yasmine's credit cards. The kicker is she's using my money I gave her to sue for divorce."

I rolled my eyes. "So what does that have to do with me, Ray? Is this going to be one of those Cat In the Cradle moments?"

My father shook his head and was about to walk out of the apartment when he noticed the photo album sitting on the coffee table. "I haven't seen this thing in years." Ray started to flip through it. He began to chuckle to himself.

I shook my head at Ray. "Since when do you care about this stuff? You were never around."

He let out a sigh and looked up at me. "You know when I met your mother she had nothing and I had even less. She was living in her parent's tiny one bedroom house on Long Island. Her room was the attic and the walls were paper-thin. You could feel the wind blow right through the walls."

I sat down on the couch. "I remember her speaking about that house. She always made it sound so cozy."

My father looked at me and shook his head. "That house was a piece of shit! But your mother was set on being an actress and she was willing to make sacrifices."

Astral Charlie flew down the hallway and into the living room. "What's all the ruckus?" Astral Charlie couldn't believe his eyes. "What the? First you're up all night crying and now you have this jackass here?" My father looked up almost as if he heard Astral Charlie insult him and then he continued his story where he left off.

"I just wanted to give her a better life Charlie. You know it wasn't long after I met your mother that she hit it big. She got a small role in a film and pretty soon the whole world couldn't get enough of her. I was barely hanging on to her when your mother got pregnant with you."

I sneered. "I always knew I was a mistake."

My father bellowed. "Bite your tongue Charlie! You're mother and I were never as happy as when we found out she was pregnant." Ray looked at a photo of himself with his arm around me. "There you are. My special little man." I looked at my dad stunned. "Your special little man? I forgot that's what you used to call me." My father wiped a tear from his eyes. "Anyway, when your mother got sick I didn't know what to do. My world was turned upside down. She was in the middle of filming and every day she was gone from the set was costing the film thousands of dollars. I had to make a decision and there you were, my little boy just wanting to know when your Mommy was going to come home. Those damn doctors killed her. They said it was a routine operation and the next thing I knew she was dead. That is my single biggest regret. Saying yes to them. I just thought we had a better chance of her being cured."

Astral Charlie yelled out. "Don't listen to him Charlie!"

I stood up. "Bullshit! You were only concerned about the money you were losing on the film!"

Ray slapped me. I held my face in shock as my father screamed at me. "Now you stop that Charlie! I loved your mother more than life itself. I would never have sent her in if I knew I was sending her to her death." My father began to cry. "Now look what you did. I promised myself I wasn't going to get upset." He began to wipe his eyes. "Look Charlie. I'm an old man whose come here to say his peace. So just let me say it."

I sat back down on the couch still holding my face. "Go ahead."

My father looked at me with red eyes. "It took getting kicked in the nuts by my bimbo wife.... metaphorically speaking, to see clearly. I have been a total ass."

I got up and walked to the kitchen to pour myself a glass of water. "Well better late than never."

My father stood up. "I'm sick Charlie. And I may not be around much longer. I just want to make sure you don't make the same mistakes I did. I'm a pretty lucky guy Charlie. I met the love of my life and even though the time was short at least we had each other for as long as we did. And we had you. If you get the same chance... are you listening to me Charlie?!"

I yawned. "Yeah, I'm listening."

Astral Charlie flew up next to Ray. "Blah, blah, blah, you sure talk a big game for someone who chose to never love again."

Ray walked over to my side. "Listen to me Charlie! You get that chance at happiness you don't let it go. You hang on with everything you've got." Ray grabbed my hand. "Because let me tell you something you never know if you'll get a second chance."

I smiled at my father. It was the first sincere moment I'd ever had with him. "I will Dad."

Ray smiled. "That's a good boy Charlie. That's all I wanted to hear. Now I'm going to go."

My father hobbled towards the door and I followed close behind him. I opened the door for my father and watched as he walked out. He turned around and looked at me and I couldn't help but feel sorry for him. "You going to be alright dad?"

Astral Charlie flew in front of me trying to protect me. "He'll be just fine Charlie. Just let him go!"

My father swallowed back the tears welling up. "I'll be fine son." My father looked at me concerned. "Are you going to be all right? The media isn't speaking too highly of you. Not that they ever did, but you know what I mean."

I sighed. "Yeah I know what you mean."

"They say you are harassing some poor woman?"

Astral Charlie peeked over my shoulder and chimed in. "He's wooing her!!!"

My father squinted his eyes and the wrinkles on his forehead began to form. "Is that true Charlie?"

I grabbed my head. "I made a mistake Dad. I gave this woman's film an awful review."

My father shook his head. "You give everyone an awful review."

"Yeah I know Dad, but I never even watched her film. I was mad because they didn't reserve a seat for me. They just shoved me in between these two overweight buffalos. Plus, there was this guy who looked like the incredible hulk who threatened to have my head put on a platter."

My father rubbed his face. "Why did the guy threaten you Charlie?"

I waived my hand. "Never mind. I don't want to re-live it"

My father barked, "Charlie!"

I scooted around the subject. "Who knows? He was probably dating one of the hams sitting beside me and got mad when I offered to send her to Jenny Craig."

My father's face scrunched up. "That's awful Charlie."

I grabbed my forehead. "Yeah, I know. But you should have seen them."

My father waived his hand in front me. "Never mind that now Charlie. What about the girl?"

I began to bang my head on the wall. "She hates me. She thinks I ruined her life and wants nothing to do with me. I've tried everything, but she's locked up tighter than a preacher's daughter."

My father stopped me from hitting my head. "Stop it Charlie!"

I sighed. "But I'm terrible and I probably deserve this."

My father turned towards me. "You probably do Charlie, but that shouldn't stop you from going after what you want."

I whined. "It's a waste of time! I'm just going to give up."

Ray hit me on the back of my head and then shook me by the shoulders. "Have you not heard a word I just said Charlie? Wake up! You need to go re-watch her film and give it an honest review."

My eyes widened in fear. "Harry would kill me!"

My father seemed like his old self for a moment. "Let him try. Don't forget that Harry and I go way back. You need to do the right thing. And if that means pissing off a few executives, so be it."

I looked at my father stunned. His little pep talked had worked. I felt clear headed for the first time in years. "You're right. Thanks Dad." I walked outside and shut the door on Astral Charlie's face.

230

My father looked at me confused. "Where are you going Charlie?"

I smiled at my father. "I'm going with my dad to the movies." We headed to a small independent movie theater near by my Condo. It was one of the only theaters still playing Alex's film. We sat down in the back row of the theatre and watched *Four Golden Stars*. When it was over I shot up from my seat and rushed home to write a review that would change my life forever.

ONE FINAL ATTEMPT

Chapter Thirteen

Days passed and I hadn't made a single attempt to get in touch with Alex. Astral Charlie however, did his best to track her every move. He floated over Alex as she sat with Samantha in Café Habana in Soho drinking a Mexican-Cuban cup of espresso, while discussing Samantha's plans for the future.

"I can't believe your leaving the show Sam. You know you don't have to do that because of me."

Sam took a sip of her coffee. "I know, but it's the right thing to do. Besides as long as I'm there Charlie is going to follow me around and try to use me to win you over."

Alex sipped her coffee. "I could help you sue him for harassment. The guy is such a creep."

Samantha shrugged her shoulders. "Yeah he is, but I kind of feel sorry for him."

Alex looked aghast. "You feel sorry for him? Are you nuts? He makes your life miserable Sam."

Sam took a deep breath. "I know. It's just that lately he's shown me another side of himself."

Alex moved to the opposite side of the booth so she could sit next to Samantha. "Samantha! Don't leave the show. You've worked there for two years. They are bound to promote you and besides... I'm leaving."

Samantha and Astral Charlie retorted in unison. "Leaving?"

Alex tried to reassure Samantha. "Just for a little while. Don't look so worried! I'll be back. Charlie may have made a mistake with his review of my film, but his bad review and crazy antics gave my film more press than I could have imagined!"

They both laughed. "Yeah, who would have thought a crappy review would catapult your film to success?"

Samantha smiled. "Okay, if you're seriously not bothered by it I won't quit."

Alex grinned. "I'm not."

Samantha pretended to wipe the sweat off her brow. "Good."

Alex jumped up. "Now let's get out of here and go have some fun."

Samantha paid the check and hugged Alex. "Okay, but this has got to be the last day I call out of work or I'm not going to have to worry about quitting because they are going to fire me."

Astral Charlie left the cafe and headed to the T.V. studio. He wanted to warn me that Lexi was planning on leaving New York. He flew as fast as he could to the studio and found me sulking in my dressing room. I was doing my best not to jump ship on my final attempt to win Alex over. I went into the station that day with my new review of *Four Golden Stars*. I looked around for Samantha hoping to get her approval, but she was nowhere to be found. I realized then that I had completely alienated the one person who could help me. Samantha was doing everything possible to avoid me, even if it meant losing her job. I couldn't blame her. I mean I was being a total prick.

I read my review of Alex's film over and over in my dressing room anxiously waiting for the production assistant to call me onto set.

The stage manager knocked on my dressing room. "Charlie!"

I called out, "Be there in a second." I glanced at myself in the mirror. "Here goes nothing." The next twenty-two minutes of my life were dedicated to correcting the worst mistake of my life. My review of Alex's film was intense. I poured my heart out on National T.V. hoping to redeem myself. The crew was speechless when I finished the review. One of the crewmembers began to clap and soon everyone joined in. Walking off set that day I felt better than I had in years.

I knew the following morning when Samantha and Alex turned on their television sets they would immediately realize what I had done. My review was on every gossip channel and news station.

The Angry Movie Guy Is No Longer Angry.

Charlie "The Snake" Evans publicly apologizes to the Angry Movie Gal, Alexis Rasner. He also made a special apology to actors: Jessica Moreau, Jake Durand, Matt Barker, Howard Gontly, Brad Morel and countless others. The news traveled fast. I heard from a source that Harry was at home in his cowboy hat and boxer shorts watching T.V. with the Smurfette from next-door when it

aired. He took off his cowboy hat and screamed in horror. The Angry
Movie Guy he'd built up was turning into a total pussy. He grabbed his cell phone and dialed my number; it went straight to voice mail.

"Charlie get your butt down to the station before I turn your life into a living hell!"

After listening to his voice message I reluctantly decided to head to the studio. Harry was waiting for me in my dressing room. The whole crew watched through the window as Harry lost his shit.

"The Hollywood big wigs are ready to sign on the dotted line and you go and pull a stunt like this?"

I sat down calmly. "There isn't going to be a movie Harry."

Harry's eyes' practically popped out of his head. "Of course there is Charlie. I set it up. Convincing Mr. Ho wasn't easy, but he finally agreed that your loveless affair was good for the film. The deal is back on."

I shook my head. "No it isn't. You can tell Mr. Ho this isn't my life. It's a character you created, which I lived by. Harry you're fired!"

Harry smirked. "What on earth are you talking about? You can't fire me Charlie after all I've done for you. I made you!"

I stood up. "No you made Charlie 'The Snake' Evans. You made *Angry Movie Guy*. You didn't make Charlie Zimmerman. And besides I own the rights to the show! Goodbye, Harry."

Harry watched in disbelief as I strolled out of my dressing room with a smile on my face. Astral Charlie looked back at Harry and stuck his tongue out as Harry screamed after me.

"You haven't heard the last from me Charlie! This is my show! You'll be hearing from my lawyers!"

I sent a gigantic security guard into Harry's office to escort him off the set. The entire crew stared at me in disbelief. The following morning I showed up earlier than usual. I spied on the crew as they moped around the studio, scared of losing their jobs. I saw Samantha walk in and join John in the break area.

I immediately raced towards her. "Samantha! You're here. How are you?"

Samantha stepped back, stunned by my entrance. "I'm good Charlie. How are you?"

I gleamed. "Never better. I need to see Alex. It's important. I watched her movie."

Samantha smiled. "I know you did. I think the whole world knows you did right about now."

I got on my knees. "I swear this is the last time I'll ask Samantha."

Samantha stared down at me with pity. "Charlie you're too late. She's leaving New York."

I sprung up. "Leaving?"

Samantha looked worried as she broke the news. "I'm sorry Charlie. Alex is going home to Medora, North Dakota."

A look of bewilderment swept across my face. "Medora? People really live there? I thought that was just something she added to the film to get sympathy."

Samantha glared at me. "Okay I'm sorry. I promise that was the last of it. Now where is she?" I tapped my foot to show my impatience. "Quit stalling Samantha. There isn't time! You said it yourself, she's leaving!"

Samantha rolled her eyes. "I told you its too late Charlie."

I glared at Samantha. "You're lying!"

She folded her arms. "I am not." I leaned in close to Samantha's face. "You are! Every time you lie your eye twitches." I imitated her.

"I do not!" Samantha retorted.

I shook my head. "Do too. Whenever I ask you if the milk in my latte is soy or skim and you lie your eye twitches." Samantha looked at me suspiciously. "I can tell the difference between soy and skim Samantha." I clasped my hands together and began to beg her. "Please tell me where she is Samantha?"

Samantha took out a piece of paper and wrote down her home address. Samantha sighed as she handed it to me. "If you hurry I think you can catch her."

I grabbed the paper. "Thank you! You won't regret this." Samantha looked at me worried. "You won't. I swear!"

I frantically dashed out of the studio nearly knocking over the station manager. Only to realize my Porsche had been vandalized by an anonymous hater, probably Harry. Apparently Alex didn't make a strong enough point on my face; someone thought it should be reiterated on my Porsche by slashing the tires. I held my hand up desperately searching for a cab. A yellow taxi pulled up and I hopped inside. I leaned forward and gave the cabbie the address. "The corner of Christopher and West 4th."

The cab driver turned around and scowled at me. "I know you."

I shook my head. "No you don't"

The cab driver smiled at me in recognition, "Yes, I definitely do... you are that asshole critic!"

I shook my head in agreement. "Thanks. Could we please get going now?" The cab driver sped off from the curb while I bounced around in the back seat. "I can't believe I'm in a cab rushing off to convince the woman of my dreams not to get on a plane. I'm living a movie I would give an awful review. This must be the punishment for the life I've led." The cab driver was within a block of Alex's apartment when I called out, "That's her! Up there - hurry!" The cabbie was about to pull up when a garbage truck angled itself, blocking my cab. I screamed, "Oh come on! I'm in a rush!" My heart was palpitating. I reached into my pocket and threw some money at the driver. I got out of the cab and ran up the street hoping to catch her. "Alex! Alex! Wait!" It was too late; she jumped into a taxicab and pulled away. "Shit!" I felt crazy as I stood out of breath in the middle of the street listening to the sound of the New York City driver's horns blare. I was about to give up when a delivery boy pulled up at a red light. I ran up to him and accosted him. "I need you. I need your scooter. It's important."

The Asian delivery boy looked at me blankly and then responded in broken English. "No I don't do that."

I took out my wallet ready to bargain with him. "I have to follow that taxi. It's important."

The delivery boy shook his head. "No. Won't do."

I held onto the scooter. "I have to catch up to the taxi that just left here."

The delivery boy tugged on his scooter. "No."

I begged him. "I have to talk to the lady that just left here. It's urgent."

The delivery boy looked at me curiously. "Lady? You and lady?"

I smiled. "Yes, yes! Me and lady. Lady in taxi." The delivery boy looked ahead at the cab, which was stuck in traffic somewhere just beyond my view.

"Lady pretty?"

I beamed. "Yes! She is pretty. She is beautiful lady."

The Asian delivery boy got on his scooter leaving room for me. "Okay. You get on." I climbed onto the back of the scooter and awkwardly held onto the delivery boy. The delivery boy drove like a mad man trying to catch up with Alex.

Astral Charlie flew full speed ahead towards Lexi's cab. "Don't worry Charlie. I'll stop her!" Astral Charlie flew into the back seat of Lexi's cab and began screaming at the top of his lungs. "You can't leave! I'm not a bad guy! And you would know that if you just give me a chance for heavens sakes!"

239

Alex stared outside the cab window at the endless traffic; she was oblivious to Astral Charlie's presence. "What's the hold up?" Lexi sighed.

The taxi driver blew his horn and spoke with a thick Indian accent. "Who knows... traffic, car breakdown, construction, maybe all three?"

Alex sat back trying to relax listening to some popular pop song named, "Summer-Time." Alex sang along to it without really knowing the words. "Ooh, la, la. La, la, la- it's summer time." The delivery boy and I sped by the cab and I caught a glimpse of Alex in the back seat.

I yelled. "That's her! That's her! Stop!" The delivery boy screeched to a dramatic halt and I got off. He watched me with pride as I raced after her.

He screamed, "Good luck mister," as he waived goodbye.

I yelled back. "Thank you," as I dashed up to her cab and opened the door.

I hopped inside the taxi startling both Alex and the driver. The driver began to yell at me. "What the hell? You can't do that buddy!"

I held my hands up. "It's okay! I know her and I just want to talk!"

Alex put me in a chokehold. "This is from big mamma!"

I looked at her confused as my eyes bulged out of my head. "Big who?"

Alex looked at the cab driver. "I don't want to talk to him. I'm calling the police."

Lifting my hands up over my head I yelled, "No, wait! Please just hear me out."

Astral Charlie looked scared as my face began to change colors. "Maybe this was a bad idea Charlie?"

The taxi driver turned and looked at the two of us. "Hey, wait a second... I know you."

I rolled my eyes. "Here we go again."

"You're that movie critic guy."

My reply was barely audible. "Yep, that's me!"

The cab driver pointed at me. "You're a real jerk you know that?"

Alex leaned back over and tried to open the door while continuing to hold me in a chokehold. I guarded the door with my body while keeping my hands up over my head.

Alex screamed. "Yes he is! Now kick him out, please!"

The cab driver smiled. "You're that couple I keep hearing about on T.V."

Alex and I looked at one another and I couldn't help, but smirk. Alex tightened her grip and then replied to the cab driver. "We're not a couple! Tell him we're not a couple."

My voice was raspy as I tried to speak to the cab driver. "We're not a couple. I made an awful mistake and I am trying to explain that to this young woman, but she won't hear me out."

The cab driver looked at Alex. "You won't?"

Astral Charlie pleaded with Alex. "Come on lady give him a chance."

Alex glared at the cab driver. "No I won't!"

The cab driver softened. "Aw honey, at least hear the guy out. Even a real jerk deserves that much."

I looked at Alex lovingly. "See?"

Alex resigned. "Fine." She let go of me and I began to cough.

Astral Charlie got so excited he nearly knocked his head on the ceiling of the cab, "She's giving you a chance Charlie. Don't mess it up!" Astral Charlie hugged the cab driver. "What are you some type of angel?"

Alex looked out the window. "Apparently I'm not going anywhere with this five o'clock jam packed traffic so go ahead, but nothing you say Charlie is going to change my mind."

I tried to collect myself. "Okay, first I want to say that I know I've been a real jerk as our driver has pointed out. And I know you thought my attempts at apologizing were pathetic, but the truth is meeting you and giving your film an awful review was the best thing that ever happened to me."

Alex looked appalled. "Get out!"

I screamed. "Wait! Here me out. I might have made a terrible mistake with the review of your film?"

Alex snapped. "Might have?"

Alex tried to open the cab door again. "No! I did! Of course I did! But if I weren't such an ass I probably wouldn't be sitting here right now. And I can't think of anywhere I'd rather be. I know you don't like what I did Alex, but I saw your film the other day. Twice! And you know what?"

Alex crossed her arms. "What?"

I smiled at Alex tenderly. "It was amazing. Not just because it was a great film, which it totally was, *is* but because it was you through and through." I was sweating from being so nervous, but I could tell Alex was beginning to soften.

Astral Charlie made a bag of popcorn magically appear. He began to eat it totally engrossed in our conversation. He yelped, "Its working Charlie! Keep going!"

I reached out for Lexi's hand, but then I stopped myself. "I just wish I'd realized it sooner because you're an amazing person to tell such a heart felt story. To reveal something so close and it takes personal strength and courage."

Alex smiled. "Go on."

I set my hand down close to hers on the cab seat and continued to pour my heart out. "And I didn't know it was about your mother and how she was sick when you were little or how her death really affected you. And for that I am truly sorry because the same thing happened to me, so I know how much pain that causes."

Astral Charlie and the cab driver began to cry listening to me bare my soul. The cab driver grabbed a tissue from the glove box and blew his nose as I poured my heart out to Alex.

I began to tear up. "My mother was my world when I was that age." Alex's eyes softened. "It was the hardest thing I ever had to go through." I turned to Alex. "I can imagine your sorrow, believe me I can. Possibly this is why when we met that day in front of the theatre I felt a certain connection to you. Has that ever happened to you?" Alex shook her head no, but reached for my hand. I heaved a sigh of relief as she touched my hand. "I thought it was because of the movie, *Lost in her Eyes*, but now I can see that it was much more than that."

Alex wrinkled her nose. "I don't understand Charlie?"

I shook my head embarrassed about what I was about to reveal. "It's sort of embarrassing, but I'll explain. *Lost in your Eyes* is my favorite movie and Jack Waters is... well, he is everything I'd want to be for a woman: smart, debonair, funny, charming, handsome and basically irresistible. And Edie Greene is everything I'd want in a woman. She is smart, beautiful, sexy, vivacious, romantic and completely intoxicating. Their life was just a fairy tale in my eyes, till I met you."

Astral Charlie glanced over at the cab driver; he seemed happy to be entertained while the traffic was at a stand still. Astral Charlie sighed, "This is so romantic."

I stared into Alex's eyes. "You are her to me Alex."

Alex interrupted me. "Charlie you don't have to continue. I get it."

I sighed. "I know I messed up bad Alex, but what I need you to believe is that I'm not really that guy. I'm not Charlie "The Snake" Evans. I'm Charlie Zimmerman. And Charlie Zimmerman knows that if a real version of Edie Greene can exist than I could actually be all those things I admire about Jack Waters."

Alex smiled at me. "So what exactly should I know about this Charlie Zimmerman that you speak of?"

I gleamed. "Well for starters...I really like you, if that's not clear. Also, I've been a big film buff since I was a kid. Hitchcock,

Coppola, Scorsese, you name it. It's mainly because of my mother that I got into it. She was an actress." We were nearly staring one another in the eyes when a clip came up on the NYC cab television. It showed a clip from, *Till the End*. I turned to see my mother on the screen. I screamed at the cabbie. "Can you turn it up?"

Alex looked down at it intrigued. "What is this?"

A female reporter stood next to an old movie poster of my mother and announced a tribute to Evelyn Zimmerman would begin tomorrow at the Guggenheim, showing never-before seen footage from the film: *Till the End*.

I had tears in my eyes as I turned off the monitor. "See...you inspired me." I said. "I never would have set that up if it wasn't for you."

Astral Charlie began to blow his nose. "This is so romantic."

Just then, the traffic in the lane beside ours began to move and a bus pulled up with an ad of me plastered on the side of it. Alex's jaw dropped at the sight of it. I turned my head to see what Alex was staring at. It was an ad for the ASPCA. I stood between Jake Durand and Jessica Moreau holding up an adorable kitten.

When I saw the ad I busted out laughing. "Oh! And I really like cats. I placed the ad to let people know how they could adopt or foster a cat."

Alex began to laugh. She had tears of joy in her eyes. "So do you have any other surprises?"

I looked in Alex's eyes. "Just one."

I leaned in and kissed Alex tenderly and to my relief she kissed me back.

The cab driver shouted, "Oh my goodness! I sat here praying to Ganesha, the remover of all obstacles, to bring the two of you together and it worked! He answered my prayers!" Then he took out his iPhone and snapped a picture. "I take one picture for memory." He snapped several photos of us kissing in the back seat of his cab and then uploaded them to Facebook and Twitter before the traffic began to move.

One year later we were tinsel town's hottest new couple and seated at the movie premiere of, *Angry Movie Guy*. The crowd began to clap as the lights came up in the theatre and the credits began to roll on the screen. I sat holding hands with Alex in the dimly lit theatre, nearly speechless about what we had accomplished. When I fired Harry I thought I would never work again, but to my surprise the Chinese film investors still wanted to make a movie about my life. They came to me clamoring over how thrilled they were to see Alex and I together. At first I wasn't sure about going forward with the film, but then I came up with the brilliant idea to ask Alex if she would direct. To my relief, she gladly accepted.

I beamed with joy as I listened to the astounding applause of my guests as they watched Astral Charlie fly onto the screen one last time. "I don't know about the guy they had playing me. He was a little on the chubby side. I think they could have found someone more handsome." Astral Charlie flew off the screen revealing the outtakes of Dr. Bloom dancing on the bar at La Mystique in his pink pumps dressed in full drag. Below him the entire cast: Charlie, Alex, Sean, Samantha, Harry, Ray, Mr. Gary Clarkson, Holly, Hailey, the blonde twins and the eighteen year old Smurfette living next door to Harry danced and cheered in unison.

The ending credits continue to roll over yet another scene from, *Lost in Her Eyes*. Edie Greene and Jack Waters stood hand in hand at the altar, staring deeply into one another's eyes.

A preacher announced, "You may now kiss the bride."

Jack lifted Edie's veil and tenderly kissed his bride. Everyone in the chapel stood and cheered. The moviegoers also cheered in approval. The scene cut back to La Mystique.

The little brunette girl from the SUV stood at the entrance of the restaurant and obnoxiously yelled out, "Hey Charlie!" The entire cast turned to face the little girl who had a devious grin on her face. The little girl put her middle finger up and said, "I give this film two thumbs up and the MIDDLE FINGER!"

Harry ran up to the little girl. "That's my girl! You're going to be a big star! What's your name again kid?" Lights out.

The End.

Photo by Marten Kayle

Isabella "Izzy" Church is an actress, singer, and writer: born in Sacramento, California, USA. She is focused on writing and acting for film, television and music. Izzy attended Marymount Manhattan College graduating with honors with a degree in Communication Arts, specializing in writing for film and television. To further her writing career she interned at DreamWorks for the head of the film and television department. Additionally, she pursued acting and Improv comedy with several of the top instructors in the country. Currently, Izzy lives in New York City and is the head of Third Culture Creative, a boutique Media Development Company.

For more information on Izzy Church
www.izzychurch.com
@izzychurch222
@listentoizzychurch